THE UKRAINIAN EGG MYSTERY

Other Avon Camelot Books by
George Edward Stanley

THE CRIME LAB

GEORGE EDWARD STANLEY is a professor of French, Italian, and Romanian at Cameron University. He is a past member of the Board of Directors of the Society of Children's Book Writers and is Chairman of the Juvenile Selection Committee of the Mystery Writers of America.

Dr. Stanley now lives in Lawton, Oklahoma, with his wife and two young sons.

THE UKRAINIAN EGG MYSTERY

George Edward Stanley

AN AVON CAMELOT BOOK

THE UKRAINIAN EGG MYSTERY is an original publication of
Avon Books. This work has never before appeared in book form.

AVON BOOKS
A division of
The Hearst Corporation
1790 Broadway
New York, New York 10019

Library of Congress Cataloging in Publication Data

Stanley, George Edward.
    The Ukrainian egg mystery.

    (An Avon Camelot book)
    Summary: The hockey team of a small girls' school
gets on the wrong airplane and ends up involved in an
international match in the Soviet Union and a search for
missing jewels.
    [1. Hockey—Fiction. 2. Soviet Union—Fiction.
3. Humorous stories. 4. Mystery and detective stories]
I. Title.
PZ7.S78694Uk 1986   [Fic]   85-91197

First Camelot Printing, April 1986

To
Susan Cohen, my agent,
and to
Ellen Krieger, my editor,
with deep affection and regard;
and, as always,
to
Gwen,
and to
James and Charles,
with all my love

CONTENTS

CHAPTER ONE

The Strange Airplane

The black and yellow school bus glistened in the bright New Jersey sun. The ice hockey team from Miss Westminster's Fine School for Girls of Elizabeth, New Jersey, stood in line beside it.

"Everybody on the bus!" shouted Miss Westminster.

The girls all clambered aboard.

When they were seated, Miss Westminster said, "Herman, start the roll call!"

Herman, the bus driver, faced the rear of the bus and came to attention. "Merridith Cabot!" he called out.

"Present!"

"Loretta Dobbins!" Silence. Herman looked up. "Where's Loretta?"

Loretta peered out from behind a seat. "I've lost my chewing gum! Somebody help me find my chewing gum!" Then she disappeared again.

"Oh, good heavens, Loretta!" said Miss Westminster.

"Carla Evans!" continued Herman.

"Here!" said Carla and Marla.

"Marla Evans!"

"Here!" said Carla and Marla.

Loretta stood up. "I've got to find my chewing gum. It's the only piece I have with me!"

"Fredonia Frey!"

"Present!"

"You know I can't play ice hockey without my chewing gum!" said Loretta frantically.

"Augusta Savannah!"

"Ah'm here," said Augusta sweetly.

"This is the end of the world!" said Loretta. She was back down on her knees, crawling from seat to seat.

"Please get up, Loretta," said Miss Westminster. "That floor is absolutely filthy!"

"Well, what am I going to do about my chewing gum?" whined Loretta.

"Okay, okay," said Fredonia, "I'll give you a piece of mine!" She threw a stick of gum over to Loretta.

Loretta stood up. "Thanks," she said, "you've saved my life!" Then she wiped her hands on her jeans and sat down in her seat.

Miss Westminster sighed. "I still find it difficult to believe that you two cannot play ice hockey if you're not chewing gum."

Loretta and Fredonia opened their mouths to explain, but Miss Westminster silenced them with a raised hand. "There is no need to explain anymore," she said. "I have come to accept this . . . this habit, difficult though it may be for me to understand."

"Well, I think it's disgusting," said Merridith.

"Yeah!" said Carla and Marla.

"Ah can't even begin to tell you what Ah think of it," said Augusta.

Miss Westminster took a deep breath. "Girls, please! As you know, we are flying to Buffalo tonight for one reason and one reason only. The National Ice Hockey Championship Game against Miss Choate's Fine School for Girls of Buffalo, New York. The championship is within our grasp. The honor of Miss Westminster's Fine School for Girls of Elizabeth, New Jersey, is on the line. You cannot let your fellow students down!"

2

Herman cleared his throat loudly.

"As your ice hockey coach," Miss Westminster continued, "I know that you've trained hard all year for this one game. You're winners and—"

"Excuse me, Miss Westminster," interrupted Herman, "but we've got to leave if you're going to catch that plane."

"Just one more thing, Herman," added Miss Westminster. "Girls, you know what it is!"

The girls all stood and put their hands over their hearts. "We pledge our allegiance to the citizens of Elizabeth, New Jersey, and to our fellow students at Miss Westminster's Fine School for Girls."

Then they all sat down to cheers and whistles until Miss Westminster said, "Girls, girls, remember, we are fine young ladies and fine young ladies do not cheer and whistle."

There was silence.

Herman started the bus. He turned north onto the New Jersey Turnpike.

"Isn't this the long way around?" demanded Merridith.

"No, it isn't!" snapped Miss Westminster.

"It'd be quicker if we took the Staten Island Expressway," said Carla and Marla.

"No, it wouldn't!" snapped Miss Westminster again.

The bus crossed Newark Bay, into Bayonne, drove through Jersey City, and into the Holland Tunnel.

When they came up into the light of Manhattan, Fredonia shouted, "Hey, Herman, I know a quick way through the city. It's through my old East Side neighborhood. You'll miss all the traffic!"

"Herman's doing fine, Fredonia," said Miss Westminster. "And please don't shout. First of all, it isn't ladylike, and besides, it makes Herman nervous. *This is it, Herman, stop! This is it!*"

Herman slammed on the brakes.

Miss Westminster hurried off the bus and into a small shop

3

with a BAGELS sign over the entrance. In a few minutes, she came out carrying a large white paper sack. When she stepped back onto the bus, she said, "I don't know what I'd do if I couldn't have my bagels for breakfast!"

Loretta and Fredonia looked at each other.

When she was back in her seat, Miss Westminster continued, "Now, remember, Herman, when we get to JFK, we're to take the bus directly to the airplane. We've arranged for special chartered seats on a regularly scheduled flight. The man I talked to gave me explicit directions, but I can't remember a thing he said."

"Oh, great," muttered Herman.

The bus crawled through Manhattan, crossed the Williamsburg Bridge, then headed across Brooklyn to the Shore Parkway.

"There's an airplane over there!" shouted Loretta. "I bet that's ours!"

"That plane couldn't make it to Hoboken and back," said Merridith. "Besides, there are a lot of airplanes at JFK. They fly all over the world!"

"I don't want to fly all over the world," said Miss Westminster, "I just want to fly to Buffalo."

They drove in circles for several minutes.

"Ah've never seen so many airplanes in all my life!" said Augusta. "Not even in Atlanta!"

"Us, either," said Carla and Marla.

"Are you sure you know where we are, Herman?" shouted Fredonia.

"I think we're lost," said Loretta.

"We'll never make it to Buffalo," said Merridith.

Herman had begun to quiver.

"There's a guard over there, Herman!" shouted Miss Westminster. "Pull up the bus and ask him where the plane for the icy hockey team is!"

Herman drove the bus up to the guard post and stopped.

4

"We're the ice hockey team!" he yelled through the window. "Where's our plane?"

"Just a minute and I'll check," said the guard. He went inside a small building. In a few minutes, he came back outside. "You can go this way," he said. He pointed to an area fenced with barbed wire. "Here, I'll open the gate."

Herman drove the bus through the gate. The girls all waved at the guard. Miss Westminster nodded primly.

"He's cute!" said Carla and Marla.

Miss Westminster cleared her throat. "Girls, remember, we represent our classmates. Everything we do, everything we say, everything we even *think* is a reflection on them."

Everybody groaned.

Herman turned right, then left, then right, then left, then right, then—

"There's a plane!" shouted Loretta.

"That certainly is a big plane," said Miss Westminster, "but it's the only one around, so I suppose it's ours."

"I didn't know Aeroflot flew to Buffalo," said Merridith.

Miss Westminster looked out the window again. "What are you talking about, Merridith? What is 'Aeroflot'?"

"It's the Russian national airline," said Merridith.

"How do you know that's Aeroflot?" asked Fredonia.

"I read Russian," said Merridith proudly.

"Why, Merridith," said Miss Westminster, "I didn't know that. I'm impressed!"

"Besides," Merridith continued, "my father flies to Moscow a lot on business. I go with him to the airport. He always flies on Aeroflot. I'd recognize that plane anywhere."

"Hmm," said Miss Westminster, "I wonder why it's going to Buffalo."

"Maybe they fly first to Buffalo and then to Moscow," said Herman.

"Are you quite sure?" asked Miss Westminster.

"That has to be the reason," replied Herman.

5

"Of course it is," said Loretta. "I'm from Buffalo and I know. Buffalo is a very cosmopolitan city. There are a lot of Russians there. They probably fly from Buffalo to Moscow a lot."

"Well, it is all a bit unusual," said Miss Westminster, "but . . ." She turned back toward Herman. "Are you sure the guard understood that we were the *ice* hockey team?"

"Yes, ma'am, I'm sure," said Herman, "and this is where he told us to come."

"Well, then this is our plane," said Miss Westminster, definitely, "because there are no other planes around." Turning back toward the girls, she added, "We have to hurry, girls, because it's almost time to leave!"

Herman pulled the bus up next to the plane and stopped. Two guards in brown military uniforms and brown caps with red stripes and stars stood by the ramp. They had machine guns in their hands.

"Do you see those guns?" said Fredonia. "Why do they have those guns?"

"To keep people from going to Buffalo if they're not supposed to go to Buffalo," said Loretta matter-of-factly.

"Ah jus' simply cannot understand why this game could not have been played in Atlanta," said Augusta.

Miss Westminster said, "Everybody wait here. I'll find out what's going on." She stepped off the bus and walked up to the guards. "We are the ice hockey team," she said in her most precise English.

"Velcome to our country!" shouted the guards as they snapped to attention.

"Uh, well, thank you very much," said Miss Westminster.

At the top of the ramp, a flight attendant had appeared. She was dressed like a Cossack. "Is something you vant?" she shouted down to Miss Westminster.

"We are the ice hockey team!" Miss Westminster shouted up to her.

6

The flight attendant snapped to attention. "Velcome to our country!" she shouted back. "Please all to come aboard. Ve have been vaiting for you!"

"Oh, just a minute, please!" shouted Miss Westminster. She turned and ran hurriedly back to the bus. "This is it, girls," she said breathlessly. "This is our plane! But come on, we need to hurry. They've been waiting for us."

"There's something very strange about this airplane," said Carla and Marla.

"Yeah, it looks kind of creepy to me, too," said Fredonia.

"My dad said the service wasn't too bad," said Merridith.

"Ah jus' don't understand why we couldn't have taken a Southern plane," said Augusta. "Ah certainly do hope they serve grits."

"I've already explained to everybody why we're taking a Russian plane to Buffalo," said Loretta. "Buffalo is—"

"Come on, girls, get your equipment and luggage," said Miss Westminster. "We must hurry!"

Miss Westminster turned to Herman. "Now, Herman, dear, we'll be back here tomorrow night at this time. I assume we'll land in the same spot. You be here promptly with the bus."

"All right, Miss Westminster," said Herman, "I'll be here. And good luck in Buffalo, girls!"

"Thanks, Herman!" they all shouted.

The guards snapped back to attention as Miss Westminster and the girls started up the ramp. Miss Westminster stopped midway, turned, and waved her handkerchief at Herman. The girls turned and shouted their good-byes. Then they continued toward the flight attendant, who was still standing at attention at the door of the plane.

Somewhere military music was playing softly.

"You know," whispered Loretta to Miss Westminster, "there really is something strange about this airplane after all."

"Nonsense!" Miss Westminster whispered back.

7

CHAPTER TWO

The Flight to Buffalo . . . or Moscow

When Miss Westminster and the girls reached the door of the airplane, the flight attendant saluted. "I am Olga," she said. "Vhere is the rest of your team?"

"This is it," said Fredonia. "I'm the goalie, Carla and Marla play defense, Loretta plays center, Merridith is right wing . . ."

Olga stiffened. "Please not to discuss politics on this airplane!" she whispered.

Fredonia looked puzzled. ". . . and Augusta is left wing."

Olga smiled. "Is better!"

"And this is our coach, Miss Westminster," said Loretta. "We owe everything to her!"

Miss Westminster blushed. "With a team like this," she said, "there's no way we won't win the big game!"

Olga smirked. "You vill be smashed! But good luck, nevertheless!" She stood aside to let Miss Westminster and the girls onto the airplane.

"What's *her* problem?" whispered Fredonia.

The rest of the passengers were already in their seats. They all had newspapers in front of their faces.

As Miss Westminster and the girls started down the center aisle, Olga shouted, "Please all to be seated! Please all to fasten your seat belts! Please all not to smoke!"

Carla, Marla, and Augusta sat down in 13A, B, and C. Miss Westminster, Loretta, and Merridith sat across the aisle in 13D, E, and F. Fredonia sat down behind Merridith in 14F.

"Great," said Fredonia, looking at the two empty seats beside her. "I'm going to sleep all the way!"

"Miss Westminster, how long will it take us to get to Buffalo?" said Loretta.

"I'm not quite sure, Loretta," said Miss Westminster. "But here comes that nice flight attendant. I'll ask her. Oh, miss!"

Olga looked up. "You vant something?"

"Yes," said Miss Westminster politely. "Could you please tell me how long it will take us to—"

"Ve'll try to be there by morning," said Olga. "Maybe yes, maybe no." Then she proceeded down the aisle.

Miss Westminster gulped, then coughed, then cleared her throat.

"By morning!" said Loretta. "Did she say 'by morning'?"

"Yes, I . . . I think she did," said Miss Westminster.

"It's only four P.M. now," said Fredonia. "I thought it would take us an hour, two at the most. Why so long?"

"I don't know, dear," said Miss Westminster.

Augusta leaned over to Miss Westminster. "Did Ah hear that flight attendant say that we wouldn't get to Buffalo until morning?"

"That's right, dear," said Miss Westminster. "Now, just sit back and enjoy the flight."

Augusta smiled dreamily. "Maybe they'll serve grits for breakfast."

"This plane must land at every town between here and Buffalo," said Loretta. "I didn't know there were so many Russians in New York!"

"We wanted to spend the night in a hotel!" said Carla and Marla.

"Well, look at it on the bright side, girls," said Miss Westminster. "With the money we save on the hotel bill, we can buy some nice souvenirs of Buffalo for the rest of your class-mates.''

"We planned to use the hotel towels as souvenirs," said Carla and Marla.

"That's terrible," said Miss Westminster. "Didn't you two learn anything at all in your Hotel Manners class?"

The engines had begun to roar. The plane had begun to quiver and quake.

Miss Westminster grabbed the arms of her seat.

"There's something very strange about this airplane," said Carla and Marla.

"What?" shouted Miss Westminster. "I can't hear you!"

The engines sputtered and died. The airplane stopped quivering and quaking.

"We said, there's something very strange about this airplane!" shouted Carla and Marla.

All the other passengers on the plane stood up and looked toward Miss Westminster and the girls.

All the other passengers were men! They had on black fedoras and were wearing dark glasses. They were also wearing black overcoats with turned-up collars.

Olga appeared out of nowhere. "Please not to shout insults on this airplane!" she shouted.

"We're sorry," said Carla and Marla. "It's just that we . . .''

"You vhat?" demanded Olga.

"Oh, nothing," said Carla and Marla. They shrank back in their seats and bowed their heads.

Olga smirked. "Is better!"

The engines roared to life again and the plane began taxiing down the runway.

Fredonia leaned toward Merridith and whispered between the seats, "We've got to get off this plane!"

Merridith looked up from the Russian magazine she was trying to read. "Why?" she asked.

"Because something is weird, that's why," said Fredonia.

"I'll say," said Merridith, flipping a page of the magazine, "and you're it!"

"Look," said Carla and Marla, "the wings are flapping up and down like a bird."

"Oh, my goodness," said Miss Westminster.

Fredonia looked out the window, then hit the call button.

Olga came running down the aisle. She wasn't smiling. "Please not to be sick!" she shouted.

"I'm not sick," said Fredonia. "I just wanted to know . . . uh . . . uh, what time is it in . . ."

"Seven hours' difference," said Olga. "Now, please to ask no more qvestions. Ve are taking off!" She ran back to the front of the plane.

The airplane shuddered, then lifted into the air.

Merridith said, "I didn't know there were so many time zones between New York City and Buffalo. Buffalo must be farther away than California."

"What was that about Buffalo?" shouted Loretta.

"Please, Loretta," said Miss Westminster, "my ears!"

"Sorry, Miss Westminster," said Loretta.

"There's a seven-hour time difference between New York City and Buffalo," said Fredonia.

"No wonder my parents never come to visit me," said Loretta.

"There's Montauk Point!" cried Carla and Marla. "We can see our house!"

"But Buffalo's the other way!" said Fredonia.

"We have to swing out over the ocean first," said Miss Westminster. "Then we'll turn back west toward Buffalo."

"Ah'm getting hungry," said Augusta. "When are we going to be served?"

"I wonder what the movie'll be," said Merridith. "I hope it's something adult."

11

Miss Westminster's head jerked. "Just keep your mind on your magazine, Merridith," she said.

"When are we supposed to turn back west?" yelled Carla and Marla.

"Please not to be so loud!" shouted Olga. She had run down the aisle and was standing next to them.

Carla and Marla shrank back in their seats again. "We're sorry," they said.

From behind her, Olga pulled out a megaphone. "Ve'll be serving caviar in a few minutes," she announced. "Please to relax!"

"What's the entrée?" asked Augusta.

"Reindeer steak Siberian vith turnips and beets and black bread vith lard," said Olga.

"Oh, Ah think Ah'm going to be sick," said Augusta.

"Please not to be sick yet," said Olga. "Please to vait until the seat belt sign has been turned off!"

"We can't see land anymore!" yelled Carla and Marla.

The girls all unbuckled their seat belts and rushed to the windows. Miss Westminster had a stricken look on her face.

"Please all to sit down!" yelled Olga. She started grabbing the girls and strapping them back into their seats.

"But we can't see land anymore!" screamed Loretta. *"I'll never see Buffalo again!"*

"I knew something was wrong," said Fredonia.

"Vhat's a 'buffalo'?" asked Olga.

"Buffalo," said Miss Westminster, near tears, "is where we're supposed to be going."

"Is Buffalo in Georgia?" asked Olga.

"Georgia?" said Augusta. "Did Ah hear somebody mention Georgia? Ah'm from Georgia."

Olga turned. "You're from Georgia? Vonderful! My father is from Georgia!"

"Your father is from Georgia?" said Augusta. "You certainly don't have a Georgia accent."

12

Olga frowned. "Neither do you!" she said.

"Yes, Ah do," insisted Augusta. "Ah think Ah talk very Southern."

"You certainly try," said Merridith.

"Are you from southern Georgia?" asked Olga.

"No, Ah'm from *northern* Georgia," replied Augusta. "Near the South Carolina border."

"Vhere's South Carolina?" asked Olga.

"You're from Georgia and you don't know where South Carolina is?" said Augusta.

"My *father* is from Georgia," said Olga. *"I'm* from Moscow."

"Moscow?" said Augusta. "Where's that?"

"Moscow is in Russia!" said Olga indignantly.

"Oh, *that* Moscow!" said Augusta. "How in the world did you get to *that* Moscow?"

"Just lucky, I guess," said Olga. She turned and headed back up the aisle toward the cockpit.

Miss Westminster leaned across the aisle. "What was that all about, dear?" she whispered.

"Ah'm not quite sure," said Augusta.

"Well, I heard you talking about Georgia," said Miss Westminster.

"Ah don't think she was talking about the *real* Georgia," said Augusta.

"There's a Georgia in the southern part of Russia," said Merridith. "It's sort of like a state, too. My father went there once."

"Oh, dear," said Miss Westminster.

Fredonia leaned out into the aisle. "I have a feeling we're not on our way to Buffalo," she said.

Miss Westminster stood up. "Well, I'm going to find out once and for all," she said. Then she sat back down.

"What's wrong, Miss Westminster?" asked Loretta.

13

"I think I'll use the call button instead," said Miss Westminster weakly. She pressed the button.

Olga came running down the aisle. "Is something you vant?" she shouted.

"Yes," said Miss Westminster, "is something I vant, I mean, I *want*. I want to know exactly where we're going."

All the girls leaned toward the center of the airplane.

Olga's eyes brightened. A smile crossed her lips. She stood at attention. "Ve are going home to Mother Russia!" she shouted proudly. "Ve are going home to Moscow!"

"Moscow!" cried the girls.

Miss Westminster fainted.

"Oh, my gosh," said Loretta. "I just swallowed my chewing gum!"

CHAPTER THREE

Princess Anastasia's Egg

Miss Westminster swooned. "How could this have happened?" she said. "All I wanted was to win the National Ice Hockey Championship, that's all. What did I ever do to deserve this?"

Olga handed Miss Westminster a cold cloth. "Please not to faint again," she said. "Please not to excite me too much. I have a bad heart!"

"What am I going to do about my chewing gum?" sobbed Loretta. She glanced at Fredonia. Fredonia turned the other way.

"Why did you kidnap us?" asked Miss Westminster. "What did you have to gain by it?"

"Please not to talk about kidnapping on this airplane," said Olga. She stood up.

"I told you who we were," continued Miss Westminster weakly. "I told you we were the ice hockey team!"

Olga smiled a knowing smile. "Yes," she said, "the Amerikanski Ice Hockey Team. You vill be smashed!" Then she laughed an evil laugh and started talking to the rest of the passengers in Russian.

All eyes turned toward Miss Westminster and the girls. Everyone was laughing and pointing.

Everyone, that is, except one woman. She had appeared out of nowhere and was standing in the aisle beside Miss Westminster. She was dressed in a white-sequined evening gown and was wearing a diamond tiara on her stringy gray hair.

15

"You got a problem, dearie?" she said softly to Miss Westminster.

Miss Westminster looked up with tear-stained eyes at the vision in white. "Oh, yes," she sobbed.

"I've got a problem, too," said Loretta. "I swallowed my chewing gum! Everybody knows I can't play ice hockey without my chewing gum!"

"Where'd you come from?" asked Fredonia. "I thought there were only men on this plane."

"Yeah," said Carla and Marla. "It was creepy!"

"I am Princess Anastasia," said the woman. "I've been in the lavatory ever since we left New York."

"Are you *the* Princess Anastasia?" asked Merridith.

Princess Anastasia smiled. "Just a distant cousin, dearie," she said. "Now, what's all the fuss about?"

"We were supposed to be going to Buffalo," said Miss Westminster.

"Why in the world would you want to go to Buffalo?" asked Princess Anastasia.

"To play ice hockey," said Fredonia.

"Yeah," said Carla and Marla, "we were going to win the national championship game against Miss Choate's Fine School for Girls of Buffalo."

"Well, how did you get on a plane to Moscow?" asked Princess Anastasia.

"Ah wanted to fly on a Southern plane," said Augusta.

"Well, you see," said Fredonia, "Herman pulled up to this gate and—"

"Who's Herman?" asked Princess Anastasia.

"Herman's our bus driver," said Carla and Marla. "He's back in Elizabeth."

"I wish I was back in Elizabeth," sniffed Loretta.

"Were," said Miss Westminster.

"Huh?" said Loretta.

"I wish I *were* back in Elizabeth," said Miss Westminster.

16

"Me, too," said Loretta.

"Anyway," continued Fredonia, "Herman pulled up to this gate at the airport and asked the guard where the ice hockey team's airplane was and that's how we got here!"

"We were only following directions," said Miss Westminster.

"I was looking forward to going to Buffalo," said Loretta.

"Ah suggested we play the game in Atlanta," said Augusta, "but nobody listened to me."

"Ahhhh," said Princess Anastasia. "The pieces of this puzzle are beginning to fit together."

"What do you mean?" asked Miss Westminster.

"Well, before you guys got on the plane, everyone was wondering why we had been delayed," explained Princess Anastasia. "Olga said that we were waiting for the Amerikanski Ice Hockey Team that was going to Moscow to play the Russian Ice Hockey Team. But she said that you were supposed to be . . . *men!*"

"What!" screamed Miss Westminster.

"What!" screamed the girls.

"Yeah," said Princess Anastasia. "Evidently you guys are on your way to Moscow to play the Russian *Men's* Ice Hockey Team!"

Miss Westminster took a large gulp of air and promptly fainted again.

All the girls rushed to her side. Except Merridith, who was trying to read a copy of *Pravda.*

"I told her something was strange about this airplane," sobbed Loretta. She was holding Miss Westminster's head in her lap and rocking back and forth.

"Give her air!" shouted Princess Anastasia. "Give her air!"

"You know," said Fredonia, "out there somewhere is another plane on its way to Buffalo with the American *Men's* Ice Hockey Team!"

17

"Boy," said Merridith, "Miss Choate is really going to be surprised when all those men show up for the championship game!"

Miss Westminster opened her eyes. "Where am I?"

"You're on your way to Moscow," said Augusta. "If Ah had had my way, we'd be in Atlanta now!"

"I knew something strange was going to happen today," said Fredonia. "I felt it in my blood!"

"Please not to talk about blood on this airplane!"

Everybody looked up.

Olga was standing at the edge of the crowd. "Is something vrong?" she demanded.

"Oh, uh, uh, well, well," stammered Miss Westminster.

"Yeah," said Princess Anastasia, "one of the girls lost her chewing gum. We're all looking for it."

Olga smirked, then continued down the aisle.

"Girls, we have to huddle," said Miss Westminster as she struggled to a sitting position. "We have some decisions to make."

"Good idea," said Princess Anastasia. She joined the huddle.

"We're in trouble," declared Miss Westminster.

"I'll say," said Merridith, flipping through several pages of *Pravda*.

"This would never have happened in Georgia," said Augusta.

"Do you think we could get the pilot to turn back?" asked Carla and Marla.

"I don't know if we could or not," said Miss Westminster. She looked up at Princess Anastasia.

"No way, babe!" said Princess Anastasia. "Turning back to New York would be an act of high treason!"

"Maybe I could pretend to be sick," said Miss Westminster. "They'd have to turn back then!"

18

"There's probably a doctor on the plane," said Princess Anastasia. "He'd just give you some medicine."

"Maybe I could pretend to have an attack of appendicitis," said Fredonia.

"That same doctor'd just operate on you right here on the airplane," said Princess Anastasia.

Everybody looked crestfallen. Everybody except Merridith.

Miss Westminster took a deep breath. "Well, girls," she said sadly. "It looks as though we'll just have to make the best of it and go on to Moscow!"

"But Ah don't speak any Russian," said Augusta.

"I can translate," said Merridith.

"Thanks heavens for that, Merridith," said Miss Westminster. "We'll be counting on you!"

"I'm scared," said Loretta.

"There's no need to be scared," said Miss Westminster. "When we get to the Moscow airport, we'll just explain to the authorities that there was a mix-up and that we got on the wrong plane. They'll probably put us on the very next plane to America!"

"In the meantime, what'll we do?" asked Fredonia. "I'm getting bored!"

"Read a magazine," said Miss Westminster.

"They're all in Russian," said Fredonia.

"I'll translate for you," said Merridith.

"No, thanks," said Fredonia. "I'll think of something else to do."

"Well, I'm going to rest some," said Miss Westminster. "These last few minutes have been quite a strain on me."

"Ah'm going to lie back and dream about Georgia," said Augusta.

"I'm going to dream about Buffalo," said Loretta.

"We're going to watch the wings and see if they flap up and down anymore," said Carla and Marla.

19

"Please don't tell me if they do," said Miss Westminster. She laid her head back and immediately started snoring.

"Do you mind if I sit down next to you?" Princess Anastasia said to Fredonia.

"No, come on," said Fredonia. "Have a seat. Anything's better than having Merridith read to me."

Princess Anastasia sat down in the middle seat.

"Why are *you* going to Russia?" said Fredonia.

"It's a personal mission," said Princess Anastasia. "I'd really rather not say too much about it, if you don't mind, dearie."

"Please to put down your tray tables!" shouted Olga. She was holding eight food trays stacked one on top of the other.

"Oh," said Augusta, yawning, "Ah was dreaming Ah was in Georgia!"

"Me, too," said Miss Westminster.

Olga gave them a strange look, then she started setting the food trays down on the tray tables.

"Yuck!" said Carla and Marla. "What *is* this?"

"Is dinner!" said Olga. "Is reindeer steak Siberian with turnips and beets and black bread vith lard!"

"See," said Merridith. "I told you what my father said about the service. It's great!"

"It smells awful," said Augusta. "Besides, what happened to the caviar?"

"Is spoiled!" said Olga.

"Would you please bring me a hamburger?" asked Loretta.

"Eat!" shouted Olga, "or I'll be back vith more!"

Everyone started eating.

"Actually," said Princess Anastasia, "it's not half bad."

"The only thing Ah can think of is Santa Claus," said Augusta. She put her fork down. "Ah wonder if he's missing any reindeer."

"Hello, Comrade Princess!"

Princess Anastasia and Fredonia looked up. A man was towering above them. He was dressed in a black overcoat with a turned-up collar. He had on a black fedora and dark glasses.

Princess Anastasia turned pale. "I'm sorry," she said. "Were you addressing me, fellow?"

"I said 'hello,' " said the man. He took off his dark glasses. Fredonia felt a shiver go up her spine.

"Oh, it's Mr. Malenkov, isn't it?" said Princess Anastasia. "I didn't recognize you at first. What are you doing here?"

"I'm on special assignment," said Mr. Malenkov. "I have been ordered to find out who's been stealing some of our most important secrets." He grinned broadly. "Vell, I to see you are finally going to the Motherland, Comrade Princess."

"Yeah, I am," said Princess Anastasia. "Thanks for the visa."

"Not to mention it," said Mr. Malenkov. "It vas to visit family, vasn't it?"

"Yeah, it was," replied Princess Anastasia. Her tiara had tilted slightly.

"An old aunt in Kiev, vasn't it?" said Mr. Malenkov. He grinned again.

"Yeah, an old aunt in Kiev," said Princess Anastasia.

"Vell, I vould be careful if I vere you, Comrade Princess," said Mr. Malenkov. He turned to Miss Westminster and the girls and added with a sneer, "You vill be smashed! But enjoy your visit nevertheless!" Then he headed back toward the front of the airplane.

Miss Westminster and the girls swallowed hard, then went back to eating their dinner.

"Who *was* that man?" asked Fredonia.

"He's KGB," said Princess Anastasia.

"A spy?" said Fredonia.

"Worse," said Princess Anastasia. "He's a fink!" She looked around to see if anybody was listening. "Fredonia, will you do something for me?"

"Name it," said Fredonia.

21

"I want you to keep something," said Princess Anastasia, "but just until we get off the plane and go through customs. Then you can give it back to me."

From her Aeroflot flight bag, Princess Anastasia took out a small object and carefully removed the tissue paper from around it.

Fredonia gasped. "That's the most beautiful egg I've ever seen!" she said.

"It is nice, isn't it?" said Princess Anastasia. "Will you keep it for me, kiddo, and not show it to anybody?"

"Sure," said Fredonia, "but why?"

"I can't tell you now," said Princess Anastasia.

CHAPTER FOUR

Velcome to Moscow!

The first light of morning began streaming through the windows of the airplane.

"Please to vake up!"

Augusta opened her eyes and yawned. Olga was standing in the aisle next to her.

"You girls vish to eat breakfast?" shouted Olga threateningly.

Carla and Marla said, "Tell us first what it is!"

"Is leftover borscht!" said Olga. "Is delicious. Is like nothing you ever tasted before!"

"What's in it?" asked Augusta.

"Is, how you say, beet soup!" replied Olga.

"Yuck!" said Carla and Marla. "We think we'll wait until later!"

"Me, too," said Augusta.

Olga turned to Miss Westminster and the other girls. "Vell, vhat about you?"

The girls all shook their heads.

"I'll just have my bagels, thank you," said Miss Westminster. She pulled the crumpled white paper sack out from under the seat in front of her.

Olga stamped her foot. "Please to eat now!" she shouted. "Ve land in Moscow in fifteen minutes!"

"Ah jus' hardly ever eat breakfast in America," said Augusta.

"Us, either," said Carla and Marla.

Olga gave them a disdainful look. "I can to tell!" she said.

"So Ah'll jus' wait," Augusta added.

"Us, too," said everybody else.

Olga arched her eyebrows menacingly. "Something is vrong?" she demanded. "You don't like vonderful Russian food? You think—"

Miss Westminster hurriedly interrupted. "Oh, no, it isn't that, miss," she said. "It's just that we . . . uh, the girls are used to something . . . how shall I put it? . . . lighter for breakfast, say oatmeal, perhaps a scrambled egg, with toast, something like that."

"Yuck!" said Olga. She surveyed the group arrogantly. "Our great Russian Ice Hockey Team loves borscht for breakfast. You vill be smashed!" With that, she turned and left.

"I have a feeling I'm going to starve to death," said Fredonia.

Zzzzzzzzzz—

Miss Westminster and the girls turned. Princess Anastasia's head had fallen down and her tiara was tilting even more, but she was still sound asleep.

"I wonder if she's who she says she is," said Miss Westminster.

"Of course she's not," said Merridith. "She's a fake."

"How do you know?" asked Loretta.

"Because I know about *society,*" said Merridith, "that's why, and she's definitely not *society.* She's a nerd!"

"Merridith, I don't approve of such words as 'fake' and 'nerd'," said Miss Westminster. "You may refer to Princess Anastasia as 'somewhat eccentric.' "

"Well, I think she's for real," insisted Fredonia.

Miss Westminster turned to Fredonia. "What was it that Princess Anastasia gave you yesterday, dear?" she asked.

"An egg," replied Fredonia.

"An egg?" said Miss Westminster.

24

"Yes," said Fredonia. "A beautiful egg."

"Let me see it," said Miss Westminster.

"I can't," said Fredonia. "Princess Anastasia told me not to let anybody see it. I think she's afraid that Mr. Malenkov will try to take it away from her."

"I'm sure she didn't mean that *I* couldn't see it," said Miss Westminster.

"Well . . . okay," said Fredonia. She took the egg out of the seat pocket in front of her and handed it to Miss Westminster.

"Why, it's a *Ukrainian* egg," said Miss Westminster. "It *is* beautiful!"

"What are all those markings on it?" asked Loretta.

"Nobody else is supposed to see it," said Fredonia. "Princess Anastasia entrusted it to me!"

"I'm sure she didn't mean that *I* couldn't see it," said Loretta.

"Or me, either," said Merridith.

Fredonia sighed.

"These markings are mostly religious symbols, I think," said Miss Westminster. "See, that's a cross, and that's a church, and over there is a fish. Hmm, I don't know what these other markings are."

"It looks like an ice hockey rink to me," said Fredonia.

"That's because you don't read Russian like me," said Merridith.

"What does it all mean?" asked Loretta.

"Each symbol usually stands for something in Ukrainian culture," said Miss Westminster.

"You mean, like a secret message?" said Fredonia.

"I shouldn't think 'secret,' " said Miss Westminster. "What makes you think that?"

"Oh, nothing," said Fredonia hurriedly. "Quick, I need to put it away!"

Olga was coming down the aisle. Fredonia hurriedly put the egg back in her seat pocket.

Olga stopped next to Princess Anastasia and shook her by the shoulder. Princess Anastasia's tiara fell off her head and onto the floor.

"Imperialist!" muttered Olga.

Princess Anastasia opened her eyes. "What thuh, uh, oh, what is it?"

"A message for you," said Olga with a sneer. She handed Princess Anastasia a piece of paper, then turned and walked back toward the front of the plane.

Princess Anastasia read the message, blinked, then turned pale. She picked up her tiara, put it on her head, adjusted it, then leaned over and looked up and down the aisle. Then, turning to Fredonia, she whispered, "Do you still have my egg, dearie?"

"Yes, it's right here," Fredonia whispered back. She pointed to the seat pocket.

"You need to hide it somewhere else," said Princess Anastasia. "Somewhere where nobody will find it when you go through customs."

"How about my purse?" said Fredonia. "Even I can't find anything in my purse."

"Please to fasten your seat belts!" Olga was running up and down the aisle shouting commands. "Please to fasten your seat belts! Ve are landing in Mother Russia! Ve are landing in Moscow!"

The girls all leaned over to look out the windows. Below them they could see the suburbs of Moscow.

The plane sank lower and lower.

Finally, it touched down and began taxiing toward the terminal building.

Signs were everywhere: VELCOME TO MOSCOW! they said. VELCOME TO RUSSIA! VELCOME! VELCOME! VELCOME!

26

From the plane's loudspeaker, the Russian national anthem began to play.

"Please to unfasten your seat belts and to stand up!" shouted Olga from the front of the plane. She had a megaphone in her hand. "Please to sing the national anthem!"

The rest of the passengers stood up and began singing. Olga came down the aisle, doing a Cossack dance.

"Isn't it against some kind of regulation to stand up while a plane is still moving?" asked Merridith.

"I'm sure it is," said Miss Westminster, "but I certainly couldn't quote the regulation for you at the moment!"

Finally, the plane came to a halt in front of the terminal building.

Miss Westminster exhaled. "I thought we'd never get here!"

"I'm worried about Princess Anastasia," whispered Fredonia to Miss Westminster.

Miss Westminster looked. Princess Anastasia was gripping the arms of her seat. She was breathing heavily.

Just then, the door to the plane opened. All of the passengers began marching out single file, still keeping time to the Russian national anthem.

Miss Westminster and the girls remained seated. Princess Anastasia continued to grip the arms of her seat and to breathe heavily.

Olga broke through the ranks of the marchers and stood hands on hips in front of Miss Westminster and the girls. "Please to stand up and march!" she yelled.

Miss Westminster and the girls stood up and began following the other passengers.

But Princess Anastasia remained in her seat.

"Please to march, Princess Anastasia!" shouted Olga.

Princess Anastasia stood up weakly. Fredonia rushed back to help her. They got in step behind the others.

Olga broke through the ranks again to rush back to the head of the column.

The passengers were being handed little red flags and VEL-COME HOME! banners as they left the plane and headed through the tunnel. They were waving the flags wildly and shouting, "Ve are back! Ve are back!"

"Velcome home! Velcome home!" came the shouts from the waiting crowd.

"This is wild!" shouted Carla and Marla as Miss Westminster and the girls were handed their flags and banners.

"This is crazy!" whispered Fredonia to Princess Anastasia.

As soon as the girls appeared, the shouts of the crowd changed. "Velcome Amerikanski Ice Hockey Team! Velcome Amerikanski Ice Hockey Team! Vhere is Amerikanski Ice Hockey Team? *This* is Amerikanski Ice Hockey Team?"

Huge banners floated above the terminal waiting room: VELCOME AMERIKANSKI ICE HOCKEY TEAM! YOU VILL BE SMASHED!

Several official-looking men, dressed in bearskin coats and bearskin hats, came hurriedly toward Miss Westminster and the girls.

"Please to tell us vhere the Amerikanski Ice Hockey Team is hiding!" they shouted. "Ve are here to velcome them!"

"You are looking at it," said Miss Westminster softly. The girls and Princess Anastasia had clustered around her.

"Please to repeat!" shouted the men.

Miss Westminster gathered all her strength to repeat, but the girls beat her to it. "We're the Amerikanski Ice Hockey Team!" they shouted in unison.

"Please not to joke," said the most official-looking man. He had on the largest coat and the furriest hat.

"Oh, I should never joke about this," said Miss Westminster, more steadily now. "We're the Amerikanski Ice Hockey Team, all right, but we may not be—"

28

The most official-looking man began laughing. The other men began laughing, too. They shook when they laughed.

Then they huddled together. They now looked like a big brown bear.

The most official-looking man whistled and crooked his index finger. A man dressed in a top hat and tails came running from the official-looking crowd.

The most official-looking man said, "Mr. Ambassador, is your idea of capitalist joke, huh?"

"I'm sorry, I don't understand," said the Ambassador. "What's wrong?"

"Please to speak Russian!" commanded the most official-looking man.

"Oh, I'm sorry," said the Ambassador. *"Vhat's vrong?"*

"Is better," said the most official-looking man. Then he pointed to Miss Westminster and the girls. "You send girls to play against our strong Russian men?"

"I'm sorry, but I—" began the Ambassador.

"Are you trying to embarrass the Motherland?" asked the most official-looking man.

"I'm sorry, but I—" began the Ambassador again.

The most official-looking man rejoined the rest of the big brown bear and it stormed away.

Miss Westminster opened her mouth to speak, but the Ambassador turned and yelled, "What is the meaning of this outrage? Are you trying to humiliate me?"

"Well, no, it's just that—" began Miss Westminster.

"Who's responsible for this diplomatic blunder?" demanded the Ambassador. He looked menacingly at the girls.

"Herman," said Fredonia.

"Herman?" shouted the Ambassador. "Who's Herman?"

"Herman's our bus driver," said Carla and Marla.

"What bus?" screamed the Ambassador. *"What are you two babbling about?"*

"Well," explained Miss Westminster, "we were on our way to Buffalo, and—"

"*Buffalo!*" cried the Ambassador. "Why would you want to go to Buffalo?"

"Just a minute, buster!" said Loretta. "I'm from Buffalo and I'm proud of it!"

The girls cheered.

"I have never been so humiliated in my life," whined the Ambassador. "Just what do you plan to do now that you've gotten yourselves into this mess? The ice hockey game is supposed to be played in three days!"

"Well," said Miss Westminster, "I thought that when we got here, the authorities would put us back on the next flight to—"

"What am I talking to you for?" interrupted the Ambassador. "I demand to talk to the coach of this . . . this . . . *girls'* team!"

Miss Westminster's face suddenly turned red.

"You're talking to her!" said Fredonia.

The Ambassador looked at Fredonia, then back at Miss Westminster. Then he began laughing hysterically, "Ha-ha-ha-ha-ha-ha-ha-ha-ha-ha-ha-ha-ha-ha-ha-ha-ha-ha-ha-ha-ha-ha-ha-ha-ha!" Suddenly he stopped. "Why am I laughing?" he said. "I am a very important ambassador. I don't have time for jokes!"

Miss Westminster's breathing suddenly became labored.

"It's not a joke," said Carla and Marla. "Miss Westminster *is* our coach."

"And she's a very good coach, too," said Augusta.

"Yeah!" said Loretta.

"She coached us to the championship game," said Merridith.

The Ambassador turned to Miss Westminster. He had a smirk on his face. "Well, well, what do you have to say for yourself . . . *coach?*"

30

Miss Westminster's body suddenly began to swell. *"We're staying!"* she roared. *"We're playing this hockey game and nobody's going to stop us!"*

The girls cheered.

The Ambassador looked nervously at Miss Westminster, then at the girls. "You'll be sorry," he said.

"No, we won't!" cried Miss Westminster.

"No, we won't!" cried the girls.

The Ambassador retreated a safe distance, then stopped and turned. "You vill be smashed!" he shouted. Then he scurried away.

"Take that, you cad! Take that! Get your hands off me! Don't you know who I am?"

Miss Westminster turned. The girls turned.

"They have Princess Anastasia!" shouted Fredonia.

Two men were dragging Princess Anastasia into the official-looking crowd.

"I am the Princess Anastasia!" shouted Princess Anastasia. "Get your hands off me!" She was trying to beat off the men with her tiara.

"They're arresting her!" shouted Loretta.

"This would never have happened in Atlanta," said Augusta.

"Miss Westminster, we've got to do something!" cried Carla and Marla.

"Oh, dear," said Miss Westminster.

CHAPTER FIVE

A Friend at the Hotel?

Miss Westminster and the girls picked up their duffel bags and hockey equipment, then rushed through customs.

Outside, in front of the terminal, the two men were putting Princess Anastasia into a waiting black limousine.

"We've got to do something!" cried Fredonia.

As the car sped away from the front of the building, Princess Anastasia continued to attack her abductors with her tiara.

Everyone watched helplessly.

"Well, what do we do now?" said Carla and Marla finally.

All the girls looked at Miss Westminster.

Miss Westminster stood transfixed on the pavement.

"Are you all right, Miss Westminster?" asked Loretta.

"All I wanted was to win the National Ice Hockey Championship," mumbled Miss Westminster. "That's all."

"Ah am absolutely going to freeze to death if we don't decide something soon," said Augusta. "Ah jus' simply wasn't prepared for this type of weather!"

"We've got to save Princess Anastasia!" said Fredonia.

"Well, jus' what do you expect us to do, Fredonia?" said Augusta. "Ah jus' simply cannot think when Ah'm freezing to death!"

"We'll go to a hotel first to clean up," said Miss Westminster, "then maybe we can think of *something*. I always think better when I'm clean."

"I could never take a bath while Princess Anastasia is being tortured!" said Merridith.

"Good heavens, Merridith," said Miss Westminster, "how do you know she's going to be tortured?"

"I know these things," said Merridith, "because I've seen *every* spy movie ever made!"

Miss Westminster looked faint.

Fredonia let out a shrill whistle. A taxi pulled up in front of the terminal building, and a woman jumped out.

"I am Tasha," said the woman. "I am the best taxi driver in all of Moscow. Please to get in!"

The girls all piled into the back of the taxi, leaving the front seat for Miss Westminster.

Tasha put the duffel bags in the trunk, strapped the hockey equipment on top, then got back inside. "Vhere to?" she asked as the taxi roared away from the curb.

"Lubyanka Prison!" said Merridith.

"No, no," said Miss Westminster weakly, "just take us to the hotel where the Amerikanski Ice Hockey Team is staying."

"Is the Greater Moscow Fancy Hotel," said Tasha. "But the ice hockey team hasn't arrived yet. I've been vaiting for them."

"Oh, yes we have!" said Carla and Marla.

"Please to explain," said Tasha as they careened around a curve.

"Ve are the Amerikanski Ice Hockey Team!" cried the girls.

The taxi almost left the road.

Miss Westminster buried her head in her hands.

"Ha-ha-ha!" said Tasha. "Is funny Amerikanski joke, no?"

"No," said Fredonia, "is not joke. Ve are going to smash you!"

Screeeeeeeeeeeeeeeeeeeech! The taxi came to an abrupt halt.

33

"You are vhat?" screamed Tasha.

"Well, that's what everybody else—" began Fredonia.

"Please to get out of my taxi!" demanded Tasha. "Please to valk to Moscow!"

"Oh, no, no, no, you can't make us do that!" said Miss Westminster. She was almost in tears.

"Please not to insult the great Russian Ice Hockey Team, then," said Tasha. "Please to apologize!"

"Apologize to the nice lady, Fredonia," said Miss Westminster.

"Well, all I said was—" began Fredonia.

"Apologize to the nice lady, I said!" screamed Miss Westminster.

"I'm sorry," said Fredonia.

"We're sorry, too," said the rest of the girls.

"Pleased to accept your apology," said Tasha. She restarted the taxi. They rode for several miles in silence. "Do you mind if I to turn on the radio?" asked Tasha finally as they entered downtown Moscow.

"Oh, no," said Miss Westminster, "why should we mind?"

"Is time for the Voice of America," said Tasha.

"I thought you weren't supposed to listen to the Voice of America," said Miss Westminster. "I thought it was illegal."

"It is," said Tasha, "but Radio Moscow is so . . . so . . . boring! Besides, how do you expect me to find out vhat the Top 40 Hits are?"

"Do you care?" asked Merridith.

"I'm hip!" said Tasha.

"What's that over there?" asked Fredonia.

Tasha looked out the side window. "Oh, that's Lenin's Tomb, and that's the Kremlin, and that's Red Square, and that's— Vait a minute, this is my favorite song!"

The girls and Miss Westminster looked out the windows at

the sights while Tasha snapped her fingers to the rhythm of the music.

The taxi weaved in and out of the traffic in Red Square. They barely missed hitting several pedestrians. Miss Westminster buried her face in her hands again. Finally, they arrived in front of the Greater Moscow Fancy Hotel.

The doorman rushed out and opened the doors of the taxi. The girls all tumbled out.

Miss Westminster raised her head. "Are we here yet?" she asked.

"Please to pay!" said Tasha, continuing to snap her fingers to the rhythm of the music.

"Oh, oh, I forgot to get any rubles at the airport," said Miss Westminster. "I'm afraid I only have dollars."

"Is good," said Tasha.

"What about the luggage?" asked Miss Westminster.

"Please to get it yourself," said Tasha. "I can't to miss the number one song! Here are the keys to the trunk!"

"Get the duffel bags and the equipment, Fredonia!" shouted Miss Westminster. She tossed the keys out the window.

Fredonia climbed on top of the taxi and began handing the equipment down to the rest of the girls. Then she got the duffel bags out of the trunk.

"Do you have reservations?" said the doorman as Miss Westminster stepped out of the taxi.

"Uh, well, uh . . ." stammered Miss Westminster.

"Amerikanskis?" asked the doorman.

"Yes, we are," said Miss Westminster.

"You must to be the vives and mothers of the Amerikanski Ice Hockey Team, then," said the doorman.

Miss Westminster and the girls looked stunned.

"Oh, brother," said Fredonia.

The doorman ran to the hotel door and opened it. Miss Westminster and the girls picked up their duffel bags and equipment and went inside.

The lobby was opulent. People were marching around, singing and waving flags and banners. More signs were hanging from the ceiling: VELCOME AMERICANSKI ICE HOCKEY TEAM! YOU VILL BE SMASHED!

"I'm really getting tired of all of this!" said Miss Westminster. She marched up to the reception desk, followed by the girls. "We are the Amerikanski Ice Hockey Team!" she announced.

The desk clerk turned pale.

The music stopped playing.

The marchers stopped marching.

"You are vhat?" shouted the desk clerk.

"Ve are the Amerikanski Ice Hockey Team!" Miss Westminster shouted back.

The desk clerk started laughing. The people in the lobby started laughing.

"Amerikanski jokes!"

"Amerikanskis are always joking!"

"That's funny!"

"Ha-ha-ha!"

"Bring on the real Amerikanski Ice Hockey Team!"

"We *are* the real Amerikanski Ice Hockey Team!" said Miss Westminster to the desk clerk. "Now, will you please be so kind as to show us to our rooms!"

The crowd stared in disbelief.

"Please to sign the guest register, please!" said the stunned desk clerk.

Steadying her trembling hand, Miss Westminster signed for herself and for the girls.

The desk clerk rang a bell and a porter appeared. He was an ex–weight lifter from the Tokyo Olympics. "I am Igor," he said. He lay down on the floor, bench-pressed the duffel bags

36

and the hockey equipment, then stood up. "Please to follow me!"

Miss Westminster and the girls followed him onto the elevator.

The crowd continued to stare in disbelief.

The elevator stopped on the thirteenth floor.

"There must be some mistake," said Miss Westminster. "I never stay on the thirteenth floor."

"Is ice hockey suite," said Igor. "You stay here! Please to follow me!"

Miss Westminster and the girls reluctantly left the elevator.

"Are you really the Amerikanski Ice Hockey Team?" asked Igor as he set down the duffel bags and hockey equipment to open the door. "Ve vere expecting *men!*"

"We gathered," said Carla and Marla.

Inside the huge room, rows of half-beds lined the walls. Military music was playing softly.

"Is nice, huh?" said Igor as he picked up the duffel bags and equipment and set everything inside the room.

"Yes," said Miss Westminster, noncommittally.

Igor continued to stand at the door.

"Was there something else you wanted?" asked Miss Westminster.

Igor's eyes were gleaming. "You've forgotten something, no?" he said. He was holding out his hand.

"Do you want a *tip?*" asked Loretta.

"Shhhh!" said Igor. "Please not to speak so loud! Somebody might to hear you!"

"I thought tipping wasn't allowed," said Merridith.

"Please not to think that vay," said Igor. "Please to tip!"

"Ah jus' hardly ever tip in Atlanta," said Augusta.

"How much?" asked Miss Westminster.

"How much you got?" said Igor.

"Now just a minute, young man," said Miss Westminster.

"She only has dollars," said Fredonia. "She forgot to get any rubles at the airport."

"Is good," said Igor. "I to prefer dollars."

"I need to check out your bathroom!"

Everybody turned.

A very old man was standing in the corridor. He smiled. "I am Josef, the plumber," he said. "I need to check out your bathroom."

"Uh, well, uh," said Miss Westminster.

Igor looked disgusted. "Some other time," he said. "I to find you!" Then he stormed out of the room.

"I hope you didn't give him a tip," said Josef.

"No," said Miss Westminster, "I didn't. We were still negotiating."

"He only wanted dollars," said Merridith.

"He's smarter than he looks," said Josef.

"You don't talk like the other Russians we've met," said Loretta.

"I'm Ukrainian," said Josef.

"Exactly what is it that you need to do in the bathroom?" asked Miss Westminster.

"You want to take a bath?" said Josef. "I need to fix the bathtub drain!"

"Oh, please do!" said Miss Westminster. "I don't think I could stand anything else not working today."

Josef headed for the bathroom.

"Come on, girls," said Miss Westminster. "Let's unpack and decide who's going to sleep where."

"I could never sleep while someone I know is being tortured," said Merridith.

Miss Westminster sighed heavily. "Try!" she said.

The girls picked up their duffel bags and hockey equipment and went to choose their beds.

Fredonia threw her purse down on the bed nearest the bathroom. The Ukrainian egg tumbled out just as Josef passed by.

Josef's face turned pale. "Where did you get that egg?" he said.

"It belongs to . . ." Fredonia hesitated. "Why do you want to know?"

"You stole it, didn't you?" said Josef.

"I most certainly did not!" said Fredonia. "It belongs to Princess . . . uh, nothing."

Josef looked into Fredonia's eyes. "To Princess Anastasia?" he said.

"Yes, but how did you know?" said Fredonia.

Josef fell down on his knees. "I'd recognize the Royal Family's eggs anywhere!" he said.

"Really?" said Fredonia.

"Yes," said Josef. He paused. "But how did *you* get it?"

"Princess Anastasia gave it to me to keep for her," said Fredonia.

"Do you *know* her?" asked Josef.

"Well, I only just met her," said Fredonia. "We flew in on the same plane."

"What?" said Josef. "She is here in Moscow?"

"Yes," said Fredonia.

"I must see her, then," said Josef. "At which hotel is she staying?"

"She's not," said Fredonia. "The police arrested her at the airport."

"What?" said Josef. "I must go to her aid at once!" He started out of the room.

"It's probably too late," said Merridith.

"Aren't you going to fix the bathtub drain?" asked Miss Westminster.

"Oh, that. It can't be fixed," said Josef. "It's just my job to pretend to fix it so the guests won't get mad. It *never* works!"

Josef turned and hurried out of the room.

"I think I'll just go to bed," said Miss Westminster.

CHAPTER SIX

Princess Anastasia Is Released

The silence of the cold Moscow night was suddenly broken.

Knock! Knock! Knock!

Miss Westminster opened her eyes. "What was that?" she whispered.

Knock! Knock! Knock!

"Somebody's at the door!" called Fredonia from across the room.

The girls all sat up in their beds.

Knock! Knock! Knock!

"What's going on?" said Carla and Marla.

"Somebody's knocking at the door," said Loretta.

"What time is it?" asked Merridith.

Knock! Knock! Knock!

Miss Westminster turned on the light above her bed. "It's three A.M." she said.

Knock! Knock! Knock!

"Oh, no!" said Merridith. "That's the same time the secret police come to take you away!"

"How in the world would you know that, Merridith?" asked Miss Westminster.

Knock! Knock! Knock!

"It happens that way in *every* spy movie I see," said Merridith. "These people are sleeping, and at exactly three A.M., the secret police knock on the door!"

Knock! Knock! Knock!

"Oh, my heavens!" said Miss Westminster.

"What are we going to do?" cried Loretta.

Knock! Knock! Knock!

"Oh, Ah wish Ah was back in Georgia!" said Augusta.

"Shhhh!" said Miss Westminster. "Let me think!"

Knock! Knock! Knock!

"There's no time to think," said Merridith. "We've got to escape!" She bounded out of bed and began getting dressed.

Knock! Knock! Knock!

"What if it's not the secret police?" said Fredonia. "What if it's just some—"

"I'm telling you that in *every* spy movie I've ever seen, this is the way it happens!" said Merridith.

Knock! Knock! Knock!

"What will you do, Merridith?" asked Miss Westminster. "Where will you go?"

Knock! Knock! Knock!

"I'll find a way out," said Merridith. "Where there's a will, there's a way. I'll escape somehow!"

"That knocking is driving me absolutely crazy!" said Augusta.

"Us, too!" said Carla and Marla.

Knock! Knock! Knock!

"Well, this is ridiculous," said Fredonia. "I'm going to open that door!"

"Don't you touch that door!" screamed Merridith.

"Calm down, Merridith," said Miss Westminster. "Maybe Fredonia's right. Maybe it's just somebody wanting to . . . to borrow something."

"At three A.M.?" shouted Merridith. "Are you crazy? You guys can stay here if you want to, but I'm getting out!" She had finished dressing and was beginning to pack her suitcase.

41

Knock! Knock! Knock!

"Will somebody please open that door?" said Augusta.

"Don't you touch that door, I said!" shouted Merridith again.

Knock! Knock! Knock!

Fredonia got out of bed and headed for the door.

"No, no, no!" screamed Merridith. *"They'll never take me alive!"*

Fredonia opened the door.

Outside stood Josef and Princess Anastasia.

"Princess Anastasia!" shouted Fredonia.

"Shhhh!" said Josef. "Please do not announce the Princess's arrival to the rest of the hotel."

Miss Westminster and the rest of the girls had all jumped out of bed and were standing in the center of the room.

Merridith started unpacking.

"Do come in, Princess Anastasia," said Miss Westminster. "We've been so worried about you. But we didn't know what to do!"

Princess Anastasia strolled in, followed closely by Josef.

"I thought you guys would never wake up," said Princess Anastasia. "And what was all that screaming about?"

Everybody turned toward Merridith. She had just finished unpacking and was now putting her pajamas on over her clothes.

"Oh, nothing," said Miss Westminster. "But what happened to you?"

"Well, do you remember that note that Olga brought me on the airplane?" said Princess Anastasia.

"I remember," said Fredonia. "It really upset you."

"It was from Mr. Malenkov," continued Princess Anastasia. "It said that I might be arrested when the plane landed in Moscow."

"Oh, my goodness," said Miss Westminster, "then why did you get off?"

"I had to take the chance," said Princess Anastasia. "And I'm glad I did, because there was nothing to it!"

"Didn't they torture you?" asked Merridith.

"Of course not!" said Princess Anastasia.

"What'd they want to know?" asked Miss Westminster.

"They wanted to know what I was doing in Russia," said Princess Anastasia.

"What'd you tell them?" asked Carla and Marla.

"I told them I was thinking about becoming a resident," said Princess Anastasia.

"Did they believe you?" asked Miss Westminster.

"I'm not quite sure," said Princess Anastasia. "But it certainly seemed to impress them. They let me out of jail!"

"Did they accuse you of anything?" asked Fredonia.

"Yes," said Princess Anastasia. "Smuggling!"

Fredonia tensed. "Smuggling? Did they think you were trying to smuggle something into the country?"

"Out!" said Princess Anastasia. "They thought I was planning to smuggle something *out* of the country."

Fredonia relaxed.

"For goodness' sakes, what?" asked Miss Westminster.

"They never did say," said Princess Anastasia.

"I can't believe they didn't torture you," said Merridith.

"I am a Princess of the Royal Blood!" said Princess Anastasia. "They wouldn't touch me!"

Josef fell to his knees.

"Oh, come on, Josef, get up!" said Princess Anastasia. She turned to Miss Westminster and the girls. "Isn't he just the greatest thing?" she said. "He was waiting for me when I got out of jail!"

Josef stood up. "At your service, Your Royal Highness!"

Princess Anastasia giggled. "I've tried to tell him that I'm just a distant cousin, but it doesn't seem to matter!"

"I am from Kiev," said Josef. "My family served the Princess's distant family before the Revolution."

"And did a fantastic job, too, I'm sure," said Princess Anastasia, patting Josef on the arm.

Princess Anastasia turned back to Miss Westminster and the girls. "Oh, if I could only get help like this in New York!" She looked around the room. "Is that music I hear?"

"Yes," said Augusta, "and it's about to drive me crazy! It's been playing ever since we got here and Ah jus' simply can't figure out how to turn it off."

"We think it's a catchy tune," said Carla and Marla.

"Do you still have my egg?" Princess Anastasia said to Fredonia.

"Of course," said Fredonia. She got her purse off the dresser. "It's in here." She took the egg out and handed it to Princess Anastasia.

"Ahhhh," said Princess Anastasia, "my little beauty!"

Josef fell down on his knees. "That egg has been in the Royal Family's possession for centuries!"

"Actually," said Princess Anastasia, "I bought this particular egg from a man on the Brooklyn Bridge."

"Nevertheless," said Josef, standing up.

Princess Anastasia sat down on the side of one of the beds and started turning the egg round and round in her hands. Then she held it up to the light.

"What are you doing?" asked Fredonia.

"I'm just double-checking the secret message on this egg," said Princess Anastasia.

"You mean there *is* a secret message on that egg?" said Fredonia.

"Of course, dearie," said Princess Anastasia. "All Ukrainian eggs have secret messages on them. And this particular secret message is the *real* reason I'm here in Russia!"

Miss Westminster and the girls gasped.

"I knew it!" said Fredonia. She looked at Miss Westminster.

"Well, I'll be," said Miss Westminster.

44

"Can you actually read the message?" asked Merridith.

"I've been reading people's eggs for years!" said Princess Anastasia. "I own a Ukrainian Egg Room on the Lower East Side."

"You work?" said Loretta.

"Sure, kiddo," said Princess Anastasia. "I have to make a living somehow. There's not too much demand these days for princesses. Oh, in the old days, I used to open auto shows and supermarkets, but times have changed."

"Goodness!" said Miss Westminster.

"What does the message say?" asked Merridith.

Princess Anastasia held the egg up to the light again. "This one was really giving me fits," she said. "I worked with it and worked with it and held it all different ways, but nothing happened. Then one day in Macy's, it came to me!"

"What?" asked Miss Westminster.

"What?" asked the girls in unison.

"What?" asked Josef.

Everyone had gathered closely around Princess Anastasia and the egg.

"It's a map!" said Princess Anastasia.

"A map?" cried everybody.

"Yes, a map," said Princess Anastasia. "Look at these symbols here. See this wide line, with the little lines criss-crossing it? Well, this wide line represents a main street."

"Are you sure?" asked Carla and Marla.

"Of course I'm sure," said Princess Anastasia. "I'm the Ukrainian egg reading expert in this room, aren't I?"

"What else does it say?" asked Fredonia.

"Well," continued Princess Anastasia, "as I said, this wide line here represents a main street, and these other little lines are side streets. Now, then, what street is considered to be the main street of Moscow?"

"I can tell you the name of the main street in Buffalo," said Loretta.

"Why should I want to know that, dearie?" asked Princess Anastasia.

"That's easy," said Josef. "It's Gorky Street!"

"Right," said Princess Anastasia. "Now, look at all of these other symbols. They represent trees. What does that remind you of?"

"A forest?" said Miss Westminster.

"Close," said Princess Anastasia.

"It looks like an ice hockey rink to me," said Fredonia.

"Don't be absurd, Fredonia," said Princess Anastasia.

"A park!" shouted Loretta.

"Exactly!" said Princess Anastasia.

"But what does it all *mean?*" said Merridith.

"It means," said Princess Anastasia, pausing for effect, "that all my family's jewels are buried in Gorky Park!"

Everyone gasped.

"That's brilliant!" said Miss Westminster. "I should never have figured that out!"

"That's a pretty big park," said Josef. "Does the egg tell you exactly where the jewels are hidden?"

"Unfortunately, no," said Princess Anastasia. "We'll just have to dig up the whole park!"

"That may be a little hard to do with just shovels," said Josef. "It's all frozen."

"Then we'll use bulldozers, too," said Princess Anastasia.

"Where do you plan to get the bulldozers?" asked Fredonia.

"I've not decided yet," said Princess Anastasia.

"What does this symbol mean?" asked Loretta. She pointed to a little speck on the egg.

"Oh, I hadn't noticed that before," said Princess Anastasia. "Hmm, that looks like a periwinkle to me."

"Those are such beautiful flowers," said Miss Westminster.

"It looks like the center of an ice hockey rink to me," said Fredonia.

"We used to have a lot of periwinkles in Buffalo," said Loretta, "but they all died."

"Say," said Josef, "let me look at that!" He studied the speck on the egg closely. "Now I know where to dig!"

"Where?" asked Princess Anastasia.

"Where?" asked Miss Westminster and the girls.

"In the summer, there's always a Periwinkle Patch right in the center of Gorky Park!" said Josef. "That must be where the jewels are buried!"

"We have solved the puzzle!" cried Princess Anastasia. "What time is it?"

Miss Westminster looked at her watch. "It's four A.M.," she said.

"It's too late, then," said Princess Anastasia.

"Too late for what?" asked Merridith.

"Too late to start digging now," said Princess Anastasia.

"Would you like us to help you dig?" asked Fredonia.

"Ah jus' hardly ever dig up anything in Georgia," said Augusta.

"I'd really appreciate it," said Princess Anastasia.

"Well, uh, wait a minute," said Miss Westminster. "Isn't there something illegal about all of this?"

"Illegal!" said Princess Anastasia. "What's illegal about wanting something that is rightfully mine?"

"Yeah!" said Josef.

"Well . . ." began Miss Westminster.

"Have you no sense of right and wrong?" said Princess Anastasia.

"Well, of course, it's just that . . ." continued Miss Westminster.

"Where'll we get the shovels?" asked Merridith.

Princess Anastasia turned to Josef. "We need nine shovels, Josef!"

47

Josef took out a pad and a pencil and wrote down "nine shovels."

"Don't forget the bulldozers," said Fredonia.

"I'll take care of those," said Princess Anastasia.

"Well, uh, wait a minute," said Miss Westminster. She turned to the girls. "We need to practice tomorrow for the hockey game . . ."

"Well, I can't practice if Fredonia doesn't give me some of her chewing gum!" said Loretta.

"Oh, all right," said Fredonia.

". . . and if we practice all day," continued Miss Westminster, "then you'll be too tired—"

"You are either for me or against me," interrupted Princess Anastasia imperially.

"Well . . . I suppose we could help you . . . some," said Miss Westminster contritely.

The girls cheered.

"There is no turning back," said Princess Anastasia.

"I know," said Miss Westminster.

"We know," said the girls.

"Once you're committed, you're committed," said Princess Anastasia.

"I'm committed," said Miss Westminster.

"We're committed," said the girls.

Everyone shook hands.

Josef fell to his knees.

"Tomorrow night, then," shouted Princess Anastasia, "we dig up Gorky Park!"

CHAPTER SEVEN

The Minister of Sport and the Golden Puck

The next morning, after a breakfast of Russian pancakes and tea, Miss Westminster and the girls took a taxi to the Greater Moscow Fancy Ice Hockey Palace. They hurriedly changed into their uniforms and skated out onto the ice.

"Places, girls, quickly!" called Miss Westminster. "Fredonia is going to demonstrate some winning shot techniques, so pay attention!"

"Why should Fredonia do it?" complained Merridith. "She's the goalie!"

"We'd be better," said Carla and Marla.

"I'm chewing gum," said Loretta. "I can do it, too."

"Ah've reached my full potential," said Augusta. "Let me do it!"

"Just pay attention, girls!" said Miss Westminster. "Okay, Fredonia!"

Fredonia laid the puck down on the ice and started skating.

"Keep the puck in motion at all times!" shouted Miss Westminster.

Fredonia shifted her weight forward and bent her knees. She drove forward with the trailing leg, keeping her skates close to the ice.

"Swing your hips, Fredonia!" shouted Miss Westminster.

Fredonia swung her hips.

"Go for it, Fredonia!" shouted Miss Westminster.

Fredonia skated across the ice toward the opposite goal, pushing the puck back and fourth with her hockey stick.

"Look at the net, Fredonia, not at the puck!" shouted Miss Westminster.

Fredonia looked at the net.

"Shoot!" shouted Miss Westminster.

Fredonia held her hockey stick firmly, brought it up behind her body, then down, and *whack,* the puck sailed across the ice toward the net.

"One point!" shouted Miss Westminster.

"Are you sure that was a goal?" demanded Merridith.

"I'm the coach here, Merridith!" yelled Miss Westminster.

Satisfied, Fredonia skated to the end of the rink, where Miss Westminster and the rest of the girls were waiting.

Clap! Clap! Clap! Clap! Clap! "Nice shot, kid!"

Miss Westminster and the girls looked up. A tall, skinny man was sitting by himself up in the stands. He came down and leaned over the boards.

"I'm sorry, sir, but you'll have to leave," said Miss Westminster. "This is a closed practice session."

"Is okay," said the man. "I am the Minister of Sport in Russia."

"Oh, I'm so sorry," said Miss Westminster. She curtsied.

"I just vanted myself to introduce," said the Minister of Sport.

"Pleased to meet you," said Miss Westminster.

"Pleased to meet you," said the girls.

The Minister of Sport reached inside his coat pocket and took out a golden object. He handed it to Miss Westminster. "Please to accept this handsome gift in the name of the Russian people!" he said.

"How beautiful!" said Miss Westminster. "What is it?"

"Is lucky puck," said the Minister of Sport.

50

"A lucky golden puck!" said Miss Westminster. "How unusual!"

"Is it really gold?" asked Loretta.

"Of course!" said the Minister of Sport. "Is in commemoration of this incredibly great historical hockey game betveen our two countries!"

"Ah am so touched," said Augusta. "Ah can't even begin to tell you how absolutely touched Ah am!"

"Us, too," said Carla and Marla.

"The inscription is in Russian," said Miss Westminster. "I'm sorry, but I don't read Russian."

"I do," said Merridith.

"Oh, that's right," said Miss Westminster. She handed the puck to Merridith. "What does it say?"

Merridith studied the inscription on the puck carefully. "The printing's awfully small," she said, "but . . . yes, I think it says 'You vill be smashed!' "

"I might have known!" said Fredonia.

"Ha-ha-ha!" said the Minister of Sport. "Just a little joke! Ha-ha-ha-ha!"

Miss Westminster smiled grimly.

The Minister of Sport turned serious. "Your being here is to mean a lot to us in Russia," he said. "Ve are to believe that the athletes of today are the government officials of tomorrow! In Russia, our ice skaters vill become Ministers of Ice Skating, our bobsledders vill become Ministers of Bobsledding, our ice hockey players vill become Ministers of Ice Hockey, our—"

"Oh, my goodness," said Miss Westminster, "politics is so complicated! I've just never understood it." She paused. "Well, I suppose we should resume our practice session. We certainly have enjoyed your visit. And thanks again for the lovely gift!"

"You vant me to leave?" asked the Minister of Sport.

Miss Westminster looked at the girls. The girls shrugged. "Oh, well, I guess not," said Miss Westminster. "When I said that this was a closed session, I suppose I didn't mean that it was closed to the Minister of Sport.''

"You vant me to stay, then?" asked the Minister of Sport.

"If you wish," said Miss Westminster.

"Then I stay!" said the Minister of Sport emphatically. "But I sit far, far, far up in the stands. That vay, I can't hear vhat you say and give avay your very little secrets!" He laughed heartily. "Ha-ha-ha!" He started to leave. Then he stopped. "I tell *you* a secret, okay?"

"Okay," said Miss Westminster. "What?"

"You should to use the golden puck in your practice sessions," said the Minister of Sport. "It vill bring you luck!"

"That's an excellent idea!" said Miss Westminster. "Thanks!"

"Not to mention it," said the Minister of Sport. He started climbing the steep steps to the top of the ice hockey rink.

"Thanks again for the golden puck!" shouted Miss Westminster.

"He can't hear you," said Fredonia.

"Why not?" asked Miss Westminster.

"Didn't you see him when he was leaving?" said Fredonia. "He was putting a hearing aid in his ear. He's probably deaf."

"Well, anyway, it certainly was nice of him to give us the puck," said Miss Westminster. "We'll use it in practice. Maybe it *will* bring us luck. We need all the help we can get!"

"Actually, I'd rather use our regular pucks," said Fredonia. "I'm used to them."

"We'll use the lucky golden puck!" insisted Miss Westminster. "At least for a while!"

"Oh, do we have to?" said Carla and Marla.

"Now, girls," said Miss Westminster, "remember what we learned in Foreign Manners class? We learned that if you are ever in a foreign country and somebody gives you a hockey puck, you should use it in practice!"

"But I thought that was a joke!" said Loretta.

52

Miss Westminster inhaled sharply. "Nothing, absolutely nothing, you *ever* learn in my classes is a joke!" she said huffily.

"Okay," said Fredonia, "let me see the puck!" Miss Westminster handed her the golden puck. Fredonia placed it on the ice. Then, using her hockey stick, she slammed it toward the far goal.

"Aaaaaiiiiieeeee!" screamed the Minister of Sport.

Miss Westminster and the girls looked up toward the stands. The Minister of Sport was rubbing his ear.

"He must be having trouble with his hearing aid," said Loretta.

"Or he may have an earache, that poor, poor, dear," said Augusta. "It's probably all this cold Russian weather. He should move to Georgia!"

Carla and Marla skated to the opposite end of the rink. Carla lined up the puck and Marla hit it with her hockey stick.

"Aaaaaiiiiieeeee!" screamed the Minister of Sport.

Miss Westminster and the girls looked up into the stands. The Minister of Sport was rubbing his ear again.

"Wait a minute," said Fredonia. "Let me see that puck!" She skated over to the boards and picked up the golden puck. She looked at it for a minute. Then she placed it on the ice and propelled it to the other end of the rink with her hockey stick.

"Aaaaaiiiiieeeee!" screamed the Minister of Sport. He began rubbing his ear.

Fredonia skated back to where Miss Westminster and the other girls were standing. "That creep!" she said.

"Fredonia," said Miss Westminster, "how many times do I have to tell you girls not to use such words as 'creep'! It is simply not proper and it is certainly not becoming to a student from Miss Westminster's Fine School for Girls of Elizabeth, New Jersey! Now, I know that since we've been in Russia, we've all been under a strain and that you girls have ignored some of the finer things that we have learned in school. But we must now put a stop to that, or we'll return to New Jersey as heathens!''

"Who's a creep?" asked Carla and Marla.

"That man up there," said Fredonia, pointing toward the stands.

"Are you referring to the Minister of Sport?" asked Miss Westminster.

"If that's *really* who he is," said Fredonia.

"Whatever do you mean, Fredonia?" asked Miss Westminster.

"That golden puck he gave us is a bug!" said Fredonia.

"A bug?" said Miss Westminster. "What do you mean, a 'bug'?"

"A listening device!" said Fredonia.

The girls gasped.

"A what?" said Miss Westminster.

"A plant!" said Merridith.

"A *what?*" said Miss Westminster.

"You know," said Loretta, "spies, espionage, stuff like that!"

"Good heavens!" said Miss Westminster. "Are you accusing the Minister of Sport of trying to find out our hockey secrets?"

"Yes, I am," said Fredonia.

"You mean, that . . . that . . . that nice man sitting up there was going to give away our secrets to the Russian Ice Hockey Team?"

"I most certainly do," said Fredonia. "That hearing aid he's wearing is actually a receiver!"

"Well, that creep!" said Miss Westminster.

"What are we going to do, Miss Westminster?" asked Loretta.

Miss Westminster thought for a minute. "Let's huddle, girls," she said. "I've got a plan!"

The girls all gathered around.

"We're going to practice to the music of Beethoven's Concerto Number Five," explained Miss Westminster. "I always carry a cassette recorder and a tape of the concerto in my purse. Every time the orchestra plays high C, we'll hit one of *our* pucks toward the Russian goal. Then I'll stop practice and repeat our game plan into the golden puck. The Minister of Sport will hear it with the receiver he has in his ear. He'll then rush out and tell the Russian Ice Hockey Team that the only time during the game that we'll try to score a goal will be when the orchestra plays high C! The Russian players probably won't even pay any attention to what we're doing during the rest of the game until right before the orchestra plays high C. Of course, what we'll really try to do is score goals whenever the orchestra plays F sharp!"

"That's brilliant!" said Augusta. "Could we use the Atlanta Symphony's version?"

"I don't think it'll work," said Merridith.

"Yeah?" said Carla and Marla. "Why not?"

"Because the Russian team'll know after just a few bars of the concerto what we're *really* doing, that's why," said Merridith.

"Maybe they'll just think we're off key," said Loretta.

"I think we should at least give it a try," said Miss Westminster.

"Yeah!" said Fredonia.

"Yeah!" said Carla and Marla.

Merridith started pouting.

Miss Westminster started the tape. The girls skated around on the ice, shooting goals only when the orchestra played high C. After fifteen minutes, Miss Westminster stopped practice.

"I'll go get the golden puck now," said Fredonia. She skated to the opposite end of the rink and hit the golden puck back toward Miss Westminster and the girls.

"Aaaaaiiiieeeee!" screamed the Minister of Sport.

The golden puck glided to a stop in front of Miss Westminster. All the girls gathered around.

"Here's how we're going to beat the Russians, girls!" shouted Miss Westminster into the golden puck. "We will arrange for Beethoven's Concerto Number Five to be played as background music during the hockey game. Then we will try to score a goal only when the orchestra plays high C! The Russians will never figure out our game plan!"

The girls cheered.

Then everyone turned around and faced the stands.

The Minister of Sport was standing. He had a large grin on his face. "You vill be smashed!" he shouted. Then he started running from the stands.

"Let me see that puck!" said Fredonia. She placed the puck solidly on the ice and whacked it with all her might.

"Aaaaaiiiiieeeee!" screamed the Minister of Sport as he disappeared from sight.

CHAPTER EIGHT

The Treasure Hunt in Gorky Park

Nine people moved out of the shadows of the Oktyabrskaya Metro Station and began walking with difficulty along Krymsky Val.

"We need to hurry," whispered Princess Anastasia. "The park closes at midnight!"

"My feet are killing me!" said Miss Westminster. "I can hardly walk on these skates."

"Me, either," said Josef. "I haven't had a pair of ice skates on since before the Revolution."

"It's not the skates that're bothering me," said Loretta, "it's this shovel underneath my coat!"

"I thought the skates would give us a good excuse for being in the park this late," said Princess Anastasia. "In the winter, many of the paths are flooded and used for ice skating. And we had to hide the shovels somewhere!"

"What happened to the bulldozers?" asked Fredonia.

"The deal fell through," said Princess Anastasia.

"Ah'm so cold," said Augusta. "It never gets this cold in Georgia!"

"Oh, are you from Georgia?" asked Josef.

"Yes, Ah am," said Augusta.

"You don't talk like you're from Georgia," said Josef.

"Ah think Ah have a very Southern accent," insisted Augusta.

"Oh, are you from *southern* Georgia?" asked Josef.

"No, Ah'm from *northern* Georgia," said Augusta. "Near the South Carolina border."

"Where's South Carolina?" asked Josef.

"Wait a minute!" said Augusta. She stopped walking. "Do you by any chance have a relative named Olga?"

"Yes, as a matter of fact, I do," said Josef. "A niece I haven't seen in years! Say, how did you know that?"

"You'd never believe me," said Augusta. She started walking again.

They had reached the entrance to Gorky Park.

"There's a flooded path!" whispered Princess Anastasia. "Start skating and follow me!"

They skated in a line, passing other skaters along the way.

After they had been skating for several minutes, Princess Anastasia suddenly stopped. "I think we just passed the path to the Periwinkle Patch," she said. She took a penlight out of her pocket and shined it on the Ukrainian egg. "Yes, yes, we did! It should be a few feet back there."

Princess Anastasia turned and started skating back down the frozen path. Everyone else turned and followed her. "Here it is," she whispered. "Come on!"

With Princess Anastasia in the lead, they all skated down the new path toward the center of Gorky Park and the Periwinkle Patch.

When they finally arrived, Miss Westminster said, "What now?"

"We wait," said Princess Anastasia. "The park should be closing soon. The lights will be going out."

"I'm too cold just to stand here," said Merridith.

"Us, too," said Carla and Marla.

"Well, we could skate around in circles to keep warm," said Princess Anastasia.

Everyone started skating again.

Several people trudged past the Periwinkle Patch, but they didn't seem to notice the nine people skating in circles around it.

In a few minutes, the lights began to go out. Only the moon lit the snow.

Silence enveloped the park. Not a sound could be heard.

Princess Anastasia stopped. She took out her penlight again and looked at her watch. "It's time to dig," she said.

"Thank heavens," said Miss Westminster. "It's hard enough for me just to skate, but it's almost impossible for me to hold a shovel under my coat at the same time!"

"Where do we start digging?" asked Josef.

"We'll start in the center of the Periwinkle Patch and dig toward the outside," said Princess Anastasia.

Everyone removed the shovels from under the coats.

"Oh, oh, I forgot about the snow," said Princess Anastasia as she surveyed the scene. "We'll have to clear the snow off first before we can dig up the ground."

Everyone groaned.

"Do we need a song leader?" asked Loretta.

"A *what?*" said Miss Westminster.

"A song leader," repeated Loretta. "You know, someone who leads the songs that the workers always sing."

"We do not need a song leader!" said Princess Anastasia. "What we do need are shovelers!"

Everyone started shoveling the snow into piles at the edge of the Periwinkle Patch.

In a few minutes, Princess Anastasia stopped again. "Well, it looks like Josef was right," she said, out of breath. "This ground is just too hard! We'll never be able to dig up the jewels this way!"

"It's this Russian winter," said Josef.

"That's really too bad," said Miss Westminster.

"Yeah!" echoed the girls enthusiastically.

59

"Maybe you could all come back in the summer," said Josef.

Princess Anastasia looked at Miss Westminster and the girls. "Do you think you could?" she asked.

"I doubt it," said Miss Westminster. "We're usually swimming in the summer."

"What's that noise?" asked Fredonia.

Everyone stopped talking and listened.

Josef knelt down and put his ear to the frozen ground. "It sounds like . . . yes, I'm sure it is . . ."

"What?" said Miss Westminster.

"I've seen a lot of underground American war movies in Kiev," said Josef. "I'd recognize that sound anywhere!"

"Well, come on, Josef," said Princess Anastasia, "tell us what it is!"

"Tanks!" said Josef.

"Tanks?" said Miss Westminster.

"You mean *armored* tanks?" said Princess Anastasia. "The kind that blow up people's houses?"

"You got it," said Josef.

"Oh, my goodness," said Augusta. "It's the burning of Atlanta all over again!"

"What are we going to do, Miss Westminster?" said Loretta.

"They'll never take me alive!" screamed Merridith.

"I thought they might be a little mad if we dug up the Periwinkle Patch," said Princess Anastasia, "but I had no idea they'd go this far!"

"Well, frankly, I think they're overreacting just a bit," said Miss Westminster.

"I should say so," said Fredonia.

Suddenly, the glare of a spotlight filled the Periwinkle Patch. Everyone was blinded.

"This is the end, girls!" screamed Miss Westminster. "The firing will begin soon! You've all been excellent students

60

through the years! I apologize for anything I've said to hurt your feelings!"

"Oh why, oh why couldn't I just shut my eyes and be back in Buffalo?" said Loretta.

Three tanks came to a halt at the edge of the Periwinkle Patch. Three Russian soldiers clambered out of them with their guns pointed.

Then a Russian general appeared. He was silhouetted against the spotlight. "I am General Chekhov!" he bellowed.

"We give up!" screamed Miss Westminster.

"Vhat's to give up?" asked General Chekhov.

"We surrender!" cried Josef.

"Vhat's to surrender?" asked General Chekhov.

"You'll never take me alive!" screamed Merridith.

"Ha-ha-ha!" said General Chekhov, laughing. "Is funny joke, no?"

"You're not going to arrest us?" said Princess Anastasia.

General Chekhov took a clipboard out from under his great-coat and consulted it. "Is not scheduled for tonight's var games, no," he said.

"What's going on, then?" asked Fredonia.

"Ve are the Russian Armored Tank Division," said General Chekhov proudly. "Ve are holding our nightly secret maneuvers in Gorky Park. Tonight, ve are attacking the Perivinkle Patch!"

"You mean you're not—" began Miss Westminster.

"Are you Miss Openski's class from the Greater Moscow Elementary School who have come to vatch us in this great endeavor?" interrupted General Chekhov.

"Excuse me?" said Miss Westminster.

"Each night ve invite a different elementary class to vatch our secret maneuvers," explained General Chekhov. "It's a sort of field trip, you know? Ve borrowed thc idea from the Amerikanskis! Miss Openski's class vas supposed to be here tonight to vatch us blow up the Perivinkle Patch."

"Oh, uh, no, no, how could I have been so silly," stammered Miss Westminster. "I'm, uh, Miss, uh, Minski, yes, yes, that's me, and these are my students. We're scheduled for *another* night! Well, come along, students! We need to be going!"

Everybody lined up to follow Miss Westminster out of the Periwinkle Patch, but General Chekhov blocked their way.

"Is all right! You may to stay!" he bellowed "You may to vatch over here!"

The three Russian soldiers began unfolding folding chairs and lining them up beside the tanks.

Everyone sat down reluctantly.

"Fire!" shouted General Chekhov.

The three tanks began firing toward the center of the Periwinkle Patch.

Blam! Blam! Blam! Blam! Blam! Blam! Blam! Blam!

"Good heavens!" said Miss Westminster, putting her hands over her ears.

Blam! Blam! Blam! Blam! Blam! Blam! Blam! Blam!

"What'd you say?" shouted Princess Anastasia.

Blam! Blam! Blam! Blam! Blam! Blam! Blam! Blam!

"I said, good heavens!" shouted Miss Westminster.

Blam! Blam!

After two hours, the firing finally stopped.

There was now a deep crater in the center of the Periwinkle Patch.

"Oh, I'll never hear anything again," said Miss Westminster.

"Us, either!" echoed the girls.

"My jewels have probably been blown to smithereens!" said Princess Anastasia.

"We'll never know," said Josef.

"I'm so sorry," said Miss Westminster.

"Us, too," said the girls.

"Vasn't that just vonderful?" said General Chekhov.

"Wonderful," everybody groaned.

"What do you do now?" asked Miss Westminster.

General Chekhov consulted his watch. "Ve have a couple of hours to put it all back together," he said. "You know, to shovel the dirt back into the crater, to replant the trees, to remortar the bricks, before the park opens in the morning."

"You mean you blow this all up and then you put it all back together again?" said Miss Westminster. "Every night?"

"Of course not!" said General Chekhov. "This is the first time in two veeks that ve've attacked the Perivinkle Patch!"

"Uh, do you need any help putting it back together?" asked Fredonia. "We brought some shovels along."

"How kind of you to bring along shovels to help our great Russian soldiers vith all the reparations," said General Chekhov. "Please to help, yes!"

"How could you suggest such a thing, Fredonia?" whispered Miss Westminster. "I am exhausted!"

"Well, if we can help shovel the dirt back into that crater in the center of the Periwinkle Patch," explained Fredonia, "we'll be able to examine the dirt and see if we can find any of Princess Anastasia's jewels."

"How absolutely brilliant!" said Princess Anastasia. "I can't believe I didn't think of that myself!"

"That is an absolutely royal idea!" said Josef. He fell down on his knees.

"Get up, Josef!" said Fredonia.

Everyone took a shovel and headed toward the center of the crater. Slowly they began shoveling dirt back into it.

"Look carefully!" whispered Princess Anastasia. "The smallest jewel could be worth a fortune!"

They shoveled and shoveled.

They sifted and sifted.

By dawn, they had found nothing.

"How could I have been so wrong?" said Princess Anastasia.

"If the jewels had been there, we'd have found them," said Miss Westminster.

"Ah've never seen so much dirt in all my life," said Augusta, "not even in Georgia!"

"Please to thank you for helping us vith the Gorky Park reparations," said General Chekhov. "My soldiers to thank you and I to thank you!"

"You're welcome," said everyone sadly.

General Chekhov looked up at the sky. "Ve must to leave now and to sleep until tonight!" he said.

"What do you plan to blow up tonight?" asked Miss Westminster.

"Is toss-up betveen the restaurant and the chess club," said General Chekhov. "Ah, decisions, decisions! Vell, thanks for the help and I to hope you students have learned a lesson!"

He turned and left. The soldiers got back inside the tanks and they roared off toward the dawn.

"Well, what do we do now?" asked Miss Westminster.

"It's back to the hotel," said Princess Anastasia. "I need to reread this egg and see where I went wrong!"

They all began skating toward the entrance to Gorky Park just as the sun began to come up.

CHAPTER NINE

G.U.M.

"Where's my gum?" screamed Loretta.

"What are you talking about, Loretta?" said Miss Westminster. She was sitting on her bed, pulling off her ice skates.

"My gum!" screamed Loretta again. "Somebody stole my chewing gum! I put it under my pillow before we went to Gorky Park, and somebody stole it while we were gone!"

"You should never leave valuables in your room," said Princess Anastasia. "You should have put your gum in the hotel safe before we left."

"I never thought about that," sobbed Loretta. "What am I going to do? You know that I can't play hockey if I'm not chewing gum."

Everyone looked at Fredonia.

"Well, what do you want *me* to do?" she said. "I only have one piece left, and I can't play hockey if I'm not chewing gum, either!"

"I don't think I can take too much more of this," said Miss Westminster. "I need to get some sleep!"

"Who can sleep at a time like this?" screamed Loretta.

"Well, Ah most certainly can," said Augusta.

"Us, too," said Carla and Marla.

"I wouldn't find it hard at all, either," said Merridith, stretching out on her bed.

"I couldn't possibly sleep," said Princess Anastasia. "I

have too much to do. I need to reread this egg and find out where my family jewels are buried.''

"I can't sleep, either,'' said Josef. "I have to go to work in ten minutes. There is a lot of plumbing that I have to pretend to repair.''

Knock! Knock! Knock! Knock! Knock! Knock! Knock!

Merridith sat up with a start. "What time is it?'' she shouted. "Is it three A.M.?''

"Oh, good heavens, Merridith,'' said Miss Westminster. "Go back to sleep!''

Fredonia opened the door.

The Ambassador was standing outside with an envelope in his hand and a smirk on his face. He handed the envelope to Fredonia. "This is something we usually do for visiting dignitaries,'' he said. "We had to stretch the definition to fit you people in!'' Then he turned and left.

"What was that all about, Fredonia?'' asked Miss Westminster.

Fredonia handed the envelope to Miss Westminster. "I have no idea,'' she said.

"Why, it's an invitation to an embassy party!'' said Miss Westminster. "How nice!''

"It sounds boring to me,'' said Fredonia.

"Oh, my goodness, the party's tonight,'' said Miss Westminster. She stood up and looked at herself in the mirror. "I'm certainly in no shape to go. Look at me. I need a bath . . . and a permanent . . . and some rest . . . and . . .''

"Aren't you going to help me look for some chewing gum?'' said Loretta.

"Loretta, so help me, if you mention chewing gum one more time, I am absolutely going to scream!'' said Miss Westminster.

"Us, too,'' said Carla and Marla.

"Nobody cares about me,'' sobbed Loretta.

"I'll help you look, kiddo,'' said Princess Anastasia.

66

"Oh, thank you, thank you, Princess Anastasia," sobbed Loretta.

"But *after* I study my egg some more," added Princess Anastasia.

"All right," said Loretta, somewhat calmed.

"It seems to me that there's this huge department store just off Red Square that sells nothing but chewing gum," said Princess Anastasia.

"A whole store that sells nothing but chewing gum?" said Loretta. "That sounds like heaven!"

"You know," said Fredonia, "I am absolutely not very tired at all. Maybe I should go along, too. I need to stock up on my supplies. This is really going to be a tough game tomorrow night, and I may need all the chewing gum I can get!"

"Then you three go on," said Miss Westminster. "The rest of us will stay here and rest up for the party tonight."

"Ah jus' don't think Ah'm ever going to wake up," said Augusta.

"Us, either," said Carla and Marla.

Merridith had started snoring.

"Let's wash up, girls," said Princess Anastasia, "and then head out. The first thing we'll do is find a tea room where I can study my egg, then we'll look for that chewing gum building. Boy, this egg is really giving me fits. I can't believe I misread it so. I must have overlooked something really important."

"It still looks like an ice hockey rink to me," said Fredonia.

"That's the silliest thing I've ever heard of, Fredonia," said Princess Anastasia.

"I think it's absolutely incredible that a whole store sells nothing but chewing gum," said Loretta.

They washed up as best they could, then tiptoed out of the room. Everyone was sound asleep. Merridith was snoring more loudly.

Outside, Princess Anastasia had the doorman hail them a taxi.

When the taxi arrived, Tasha jumped out.

"Hey, Tasha!" said the girls.

"Hey yourself, kids!" said Tasha. The radio was on and Tasha was snapping her fingers to the rhythm of the music. "Vhere to?" she asked.

"Can you recommend a good tea room?" said Princess Anastasia.

"I to know a good tea room in Red Square," said Tasha. "All the taxi drivers use it. Please to get in!"

Princess Anastasia and the girls got inside the taxi. Tasha roared off toward Red Square, scattering pedestrians in her wake.

Finally, they arrived.

"Knock three times and ask for Yuri," said Tasha. "Tell him I sent you!"

"Thanks, Tasha!" said Fredonia. "How much?"

"My treat!" said Tasha as she roared away from the curb.

The three walked up to the tea room door. Princess Anastasia knocked three times.

A sliding panel opened. "Vell," said a voice, "vhat is it you vant?"

"Tasha sent us," said Princess Anastasia. "Take us to Yuri!"

The door to the tea room opened.

"I am Yuri," said the man. "Please to follow me!"

Yuri led them into the darkened tea room and seated them next to a silver samovar.

"Three teas and a newspaper," said Princess Anastasia.

"Coming up," said Yuri.

"Why a newspaper?" asked Fredonia.

"People always read newspapers in tea rooms," said Princess Anastasia. "You two can read the newspaper. I'll read my egg."

"But I don't read Russian," said Loretta.

"Me, either," said Fredonia.

"Pretend!" said Princess Anastasia. "I don't have time to read it to you!"

"Merridith should have come along," said Loretta.

"I'll pretend!" said Fredonia.

Yuri arrived with three cups of steaming tea and a newspaper. Princess Anastasia pushed the newspaper over to Fredonia and Loretta, then started to take the Ukrainian egg out of her purse; then she stopped and pulled the newspaper back to her.

"What's wrong?" asked Fredonia.

"Look at this!" said Princess Anastasia, pointing to an article on the front page. "It's a story about people smuggling things out of Russia."

"That's what they thought you were doing, isn't it?" said Loretta.

"Yes, it is," said Princess Anastasia, "and just listen to what it is that people are smuggling out!"

"What?" said Loretta.

"The game plans of the Russian Ice Hockey Team!" said Princess Anastasia.

"What?" said Fredonia. "Let me see that!" Princess Anastasia pushed the newspaper over to her. Fredonia looked at the article. "I can't read this!" she said. She pushed the newspaper back to Princess Anastasia. "What does it say?"

"It says that the Russian police are looking for the person who has been smuggling the secret game plans of the Russian Ice Hockey Team out of Russia and then selling them to the highest bidder," said Princess Anastasia. "The game plans have turned up on all kinds of things. They've been embroidered onto bath towels, stenciled onto ties, and decorated on cakes. But the police have no idea who's been doing it."

"Boy, if we could find one of those towels or ties or cakes," said Loretta, "we'd beat the Russians for sure!"

"Fat chance!" said Fredonia.

Princess Anastasia sighed. "Oh, well," she said. She pushed the newspaper back over to the girls, then took the

69

Ukrainian egg out of her purse and started examining it. "This egg holds the secret to my family treasure. I simply must figure out what it says!" She took a sip of tea. "This is depressing. I've never had an egg give me so much trouble before. Usually, I can read one of these things in a matter of minutes."

While Princess Anastasia studied the Ukrainian egg, the girls pretended to read the newspaper.

Finally, Princess Anastasia said, "I'm getting a headache. Let's go."

They all got up.

Yuri rushed to the table. "Please to pay!" he said.

"I only have dollars," said Princess Anastasia. "I don't have any rubles."

"Is all right," said Yuri.

Princess Anastasia and the girls left the tea room and headed into Red Square.

"Now, to find that department store," said Princess Anastasia. "I'm sure it was somewhere around here. I remember seeing it when I was attacking that man with my tiara on the way to jail."

They walked farther into Red Square, looking around them.

"I'm just sure . . . there it is!" shouted Princess Anastasia. "Over there on October 25th Street!"

The girls looked. Towering above them was a huge building. On the front of the building were the letters G.U.M.

"Oh, wait till I tell the people back in Buffalo about this!" said Loretta. "Just think, a whole store with nothing but chewing gum for sale."

"What'd I tell you?" said Princess Anastasia.

"Come on," said Fredonia. "Let's go see what flavors they have!"

They entered the department store.

Chandeliers hung from the vaulted ceilings. A fountain shot water high into the air.

"This place looks like a palace!" said Loretta.

70

"I feel right at home," said Princess Anastasia.

"It looks like a mall in Westchester County to me," said Fredonia.

They began looking in all the shop windows.

"Where's the gum?" said Fredonia. "I see everything else in here but chewing gum!"

The shop windows were full of wood carvings, furs, long-playing records, musical instruments, lacework, and rugs.

"I feel an anxiety attack coming on," said Loretta. "There had better be some place around here that sells chewing gum!"

"I'll ask around," said Princess Anastasia. She approached a *babushka* holding a dust cloth and a broom. "Excuse me," she said. "Could you please tell me where they sell chewing gum around here?"

The *babushka* looked up. Then she turned and pointed to the end of the long passageway. "Is the cheving gum shop down there!" she said.

"I thought this whole building was full of chewing gum," said Loretta. "I'm disappointed!"

"Oh, in the old days, before the Revolution, it vas," said the *babushka* sadly. "In fact, they've never even gotten around to changing the sign on the outside of the building. But times have changed, and ve've had to branch out to meet the demands of the peasants. Oh, I to remember the Czar and the Czarina pulling up in front of this store in their magnificent carriages and spending the whole day shopping for cheving gum!" The *babushka* paused. She seemed to notice Princess Anastasia for the first time. "I must to be dreaming," she said. "They looked just like you!" She fell to her knees.

"Please get up!" said Princess Anastasia.

The *babushka* stood up. "Now look at them," she continued. Her hand made a sweeping motion of the entire building. "Rabble!" she shouted. Then she lowered her head again and went back to sweeping.

"Come along, girls," said Princess Anastasia.

71

They headed toward a small shop at the end of the long passageway. The windows of the shop were stacked high with packages of chewing gum.

"At last!" shouted Loretta.

"We won't have any trouble winning that game now!" said Fredonia.

They entered the shop. A bell on the door jangled.

"Is something you vant?" shouted a voice from behind the counter. Then the owner of the voice stood up.

"Olga!" shouted everyone.

"Please to tell me if you have been smashed yet!" said Olga.

"No," said Fredonia. "That's why we're here! We need some chewing gum. The big game is tomorrow night and we can't play hockey if we're not chewing gum!"

Olga smirked. "You *vill* be smashed!"

"What are you doing working here?" asked Loretta. "Don't you fly anymore?"

"I vas fired!" said Olga sadly.

"Oh, that's too bad," said Princess Anastasia. "Why?"

"They found a better Cossack dancer!" replied Olga. "But not to vorry! I vas ready for a promotion, anyvay! This is the best cheving gum shop in all of Moscow!"

"What flavors do you sell?" asked Loretta.

"Ve have all the popular flavors," said Olga.

"Do you have peppermint?" asked Fredonia.

"Do you have spearmint?" asked Loretta.

"Yuck!" said Olga. "No respectable Russian vould to chew that!"

"Well, what flavors do you have, then?" asked Fredonia.

"This purple one over here is beet," said Olga.

"Yuck!" said Fredonia.

"What flavor is this light green one?" asked Loretta.

Olga looked. "Is my favorite!" she said. "Is cabbage! Vant to try a piece?"

72

"Maybe later," said Loretta.

"Don't you have any normal flavors?" asked Fredonia.

"Vell, ve sell a lot of this vhite one over here," said Olga.

"What flavor is that one?" asked Princess Anastasia.

"Is garlic," said Olga. "Is good for the vampires that come in from Transylvania."

"What's this brown one over here?" asked Fredonia.

"Is tea," said Olga, "but it stains your teeth!"

"I have a feeling we're going to lose this game after all," whispered Loretta to Fredonia.

"I'm not giving up yet," said Fredonia. "What flavor is this red one here, Olga?"

"Hmm," said Olga. "Oh, yes, is red caviar, and behind that one are two of our new flavors, sour cream and red pepper."

"Okay," said Fredonia, "I'll take one package of sour cream and one of tea."

"I'll take a package of red pepper and one of cabbage," said Loretta. "I don't want to stain my beautiful teeth!"

"Vell, vhat about you, Princess Anastasia?" said Olga. "Vhat flavors do you vant?"

"Princesses don't usually chew gum," said Princess Anastasia, "but I think I shall take a package of that red caviar."

"Is good," said Olga. "Please to pay now!"

"I only have dollars," said Fredonia. "No rubles."

"Is also good," said Olga.

"Oh, say, I almost forgot to tell you something exciting, Olga!" said Loretta.

"Vhat?" said Olga.

"We met your Uncle Josef the other day!" said Loretta.

"Uncle *Josef!*" cried Olga. Her eyes began to mist over. "It has been so long since I've seen him. Please to tell me vhere he is!"

"He works at the Greater Moscow Fancy Hotel," said Fredonia. "He pretends to repair the plumbing there."

"I alvays knew that he vould be successful," said Olga. "Please, I must to see him!"

"I have an idea," said Princess Anastasia. "He'll be at the big ice hockey game tomorrow night. Why don't you meet us there and you two can have a reunion!"

"Is vonderful idea!" said Olga. She handed them their packages of chewing gum. "Please to enjoy!"

"Until tomorrow night, then," said Princess Anastasia.

Olga nodded.

They turned and started to leave the shop.

"Please to vait!" shouted Olga. Princess Anastasia and the girls turned around. "Please not to be smashed too much!" said Olga. Then she smiled.

CHAPTER TEN

The Party at the Embassy

The wooden sign in front of the old building said:

TEMPORARY AMERIKANSKI EMBASSY
Please Excuse Us While We Remodel
Look for the Reopening Soon of Our Beautiful New
Bug-Proof Building!

"This must be the place!" said Fredonia.

Miss Westminster walked up on the front porch and rang the bell. A butler opened the door, and everyone walked inside.

"Good evening," said the Ambassador icily when he saw Miss Westminster and the girls.

"Good evening," said the girls.

Miss Westminster curtsied.

"Please don't do that!" shouted the Ambassador. "We discourage that type of behavior abroad!"

Princess Anastasia held out her hand to be kissed.

The Ambassador looked up. "Who are you? Do you have an invitation?"

"I'm here on theirs," said Princess Anastasia. She waved her hand back and forth in front of the Ambassador's nose. "I was in the room when you delivered the invitation."

"Well, whatever," said the Ambassador. He lifted his nose into the air and away from Princess Anastasia's hand. "Please hurry along. You're holding up the receiving line." With that, he scurried away.

"What a snob!" said Loretta.

"I bet he doesn't have a drop of blue blood in his veins," said Merridith.

"I've had butlers with more class," said Princess Anastasia.

"Where's the food?" asked Carla and Marla.

"Over there," said Augusta. She pointed to several long tables across the ballroom.

"Well, let's forget about this receiving line and go dig in, then!" said Fredonia.

"I'm with you," said Princess Anastasia.

"Well, we really should stay and—" Miss Westminster started to say, but everyone had already rushed across the ballroom to the buffet tables.

"Look at all that fresh fruit!" said Carla and Marla.

"Yeah," said Fredonia, "and in the middle of winter, too."

"Where'd it all come from, I wonder?" said Princess Anastasia.

"It vas shipped in the diplomatic pouch this morning," whispered a voice.

Everyone looked up. A server behind one of the tables was grinning at them.

"Really?" said Miss Westminster. "How nice!"

"Not so nice," whispered the server. "The grapes vere sqvashed all over some of the Ambassador's secret telegrams. He vas furious!"

"I can imagine," said Miss Westminster. "Those telegrams were probably very important."

"Oh, he didn't care about the telegrams," whispered the server. "He vas mad about the grapes. He's crazy for grapes!"

"Do you have any fried chicken and black-eyed peas?" asked Augusta.

"I to beg your pardon?" whispered the server. "Please to explain!"

"Ah'm talking soul food," said Augusta. "Ah haven't had any good Southern cooking since Ah've been here and Ah'm about to starve to death! Ah know Ah've lost at least ten pounds. Ah'll probably be too weak to play the Russians!"

"Ohhhh!" whispered the server. "You are the Amerikanskis here to play the ice hockey game?"

"That's right," said Miss Westminster.

"Please to be quiet, then!" whispered the server. "This room is bugged!"

"What are you talking about?" asked Princess Anastasia.

"I to mean that there are listening devices in the valls of the Temporary Embassy," whispered the server. "They can to hear everything you say! That's vhy I'm vhispering!"

"They'll never take me alive!" screamed Merridith.

Everyone in the ballroom turned and looked at the girls.

"Keep quiet, Merridith!" said Miss Westminster through clenched teeth. She turned toward the people in the room and smiled apologetically. Everyone smiled back, then continued talking and eating. "I suppose they're still trying to find out our hockey secrets," whispered Miss Westminster to the server.

"Who cares about hockey secrets!" whispered the server. "They vant to know vhere ve get our fresh fruit. Important things first!"

"Surely there are more important things to learn than where the fresh fruit comes from," said Miss Westminster. "I'm disillusioned!"

The server inhaled sharply. His expression hardened. "You vould never make it in the diplomatic vorld!" he shouted, then turned and began rearranging the strawberries.

"The people here certainly are strange, aren't they?" said Carla and Marla.

"Girls, girls!" whispered Miss Westminster. "Don't forget

77

what we learned in our Embassy Party Manners class. We learned that if you are ever invited to an embassy party, you should make the most of it!''

''That's very good advice, girls,'' said Princess Anastasia.

The girls groaned.

Finally, with plates piled high with food, everyone started looking for a place to sit down and eat.

After two complete circles of the ballroom, Miss Westminster said, ''Maybe we can find a place to eat somewhere upstairs.''

''Good idea!'' said Fredonia.

They found the stairs and started climbing.

When they reached the second floor, Loretta said, ''Well, where do we go from here?''

''Here's a room down here we can eat in!'' said Princess Anastasia. ''The door's open and there's nobody around to bother us!''

Miss Westminster stuck her head inside the door. ''It's kind of drab, isn't it, what with all those filing cabinets and desks, and all that radio and teletype equipment? Couldn't we look for a place a little more cheerful?''

''Ah'm hungry,'' said Augusta. ''Ah want to eat now!''

''Us, too,'' said Carla and Marla.

''Look at that sign,'' said Merridith, pointing. ''It says CODE ROOM! ENTRY FORBIDDEN! THAT MEANS YOU!''

''I'm sure they must be talking about the Russians,'' said Loretta. ''They couldn't possibly mean us. We're Americans!''

''Yeah!'' said Carla and Marla.

''Let's just go inside and eat!'' said Fredonia.

''Well, I guess it's all right,'' said Miss Westminster.

''Sure it is, dearie,'' said Princess Anastasia.

Everyone went inside the room and found a chair and sat down.

''Hey, look at this!'' said Loretta. She picked up a file folder

78

from the counter and knocked her egg salad off onto the floor. "Oh, yuck!"

"Clean up your mess, Loretta!" said Miss Westminster.

"What does it say?" asked Fredonia.

"It says 'Top Secret,' " said Loretta.

"Oh, it's probably just something that the Ambassador doesn't want his wife to find out about, that's all!" said Merridith.

"Oh, I don't know about that," said Loretta. "Listen to this: 'The Russian Prime Minister has requested political asylum in America. It has been denied!' "

"*Aaaaaiiiiieeeee!*"

Everyone looked up. A man was standing in the doorway. His mouth was open and he was screaming. Then he stopped screaming and started shouting, "Out! Out! Out! Out! Out! Out! Out! Out! Out! Out! Out! Out!"

"Good heavens, young man!" said Miss Westminster. "Get hold of yourself!"

"Hey, look at *this!*" said Fredonia. She pushed away a stack of towels, men's ties, and a carton of eggs. "Here's another file stamped 'Top Secret'!"

"*Don't you touch that file!*" screamed the man again. He lunged for Fredonia, but Fredonia moved quickly out of the way. The man slipped on Loretta's egg salad and fell to the floor.

"*Oh, my heavens!*" screamed Miss Westminster. "*He's dead!*"

But the man slowly lifted his head off the floor. "How . . . did . . . you . . . people . . . get . . . in . . . here?" he asked weakly.

"We walked in," said Loretta.

"But . . . the . . . door . . . was . . . oh, my heavens . . . did . . . I . . . leave . . . that . . . door . . . open . . . again?" The man sat up slowly and rubbed his head. "I . . . only went . . . downstairs . . . to get a . . . cup of coffee. I had . . . no idea . . . anybody would . . ." He looked around the room, then he used the arm of a chair to pull himself off the floor. When he was finally standing, he started shouting again, "Get out! Get out! Get out! Get out! Get out! Get out!"

"All right, already!" screamed Princess Anastasia back. *"We're going!"*

Loretta hurriedly picked up her plate from the counter. The chopped banana fell into the teletype machine. It stopped teletyping.

"What have you done *now?*" shouted the man. "Out! Out! Out! Out! Out! Out! Out! Out! Out! Out! Out!"

When everyone was out of the room, the man slammed the door.

"You can't treat us that way!" shouted Loretta. "We're Americans!"

"How rude!" said Miss Westminster. "We'll just have to go back downstairs to the party and pretend that none of this happened!"

"Ah'm ready to leave," said Augusta.

"Yeah!" echoed the girls. "We're ready to leave, too!"

"Men most certainly don't act like that in Atlanta!" Augusta added.

They met the Ambassador coming up the stairs. "What was all that shouting about?" he said. "What's wrong?"

"That man in the Code Room was rude to us!" said Merridith.

"You were in the *Code* Room?" shouted the Ambassador.

"Yes," said Loretta, "and personally, I think it's disgraceful that you won't let the Russian Prime Minister defect if he wants to!"

The Ambassador turned pale. "What . . . what . . . what . . . what are you talking about?" he screamed. "Did you . . . did you . . . did you . . . how did you know . . . how did you know . . . how . . . how . . . how?"

"I read the secret file," said Loretta calmly.

"You read *what?*" screamed the Ambassador.

"Come along, girls," said Miss Westminster. "We must be going."

"You idiots!" screamed the Ambassador. "First you embarrass me by coming here to play a hockey game against the Russian *Men's* Ice Hockey Team, and now you break all kinds of security regulations by reading the secret files!"

"I'll have no more of this peasant's insolence!" said Princess Anastasia. She began sweeping through the ballroom, followed hurriedly by Miss Westminster and the girls.

The other guests had stopped eating and talking to watch.

"I think you're all spies!" the Ambassador continued to scream. "My career is ruined! What did I ever do to deserve this?"

The butler opened the door for everyone, then slammed it shut.

"Ah never thought Ah'd enjoy being outside in this cold air," said Augusta, "but Ah most certainly do!"

"Fredonia, what do you have in your hand?" asked Miss Westminster.

"It's a file folder I picked up in the Code Room," replied Fredonia.

"What?" said Miss Westminster. "You mean you stole a secret document?"

"No, I didn't *steal* it," said Fredonia. "I just *borrowed* it, because I wasn't through reading it."

"You could be in serious trouble if you take that document," said Merridith. "They'll put us in prison and it'll all be because of you, but *they'll never take me alive!*"

"I don't plan to keep it," said Fredonia. "I plan to return it in just a few minutes. Right after I've finished it. Here, look at this!" Everyone gathered around. "Do these markings on this paper look familiar?"

Everyone looked closely.

"Why, yes, they do," said Princess Anastasia. "I've seen those markings before. But I can't remember where!"

"Say," said Miss Westminster, "aren't those the same markings on that Ukrainian egg of yours, Princess Anastasia?"

"Well, I do believe they are!" said Princess Anastasia. "What does this mean?"

"Look at the label on this file," said Fredonia. She held it up so everyone could see it. " 'Secret Game Plans of the Russian Ice Hockey Team'!"

"What?" said Miss Westminster. "Do you mean that those markings on Princess Anastasia's egg are the game plans of the Russian Ice Hockey Team?"

"They most certainly are!" said Fredonia.

"You mean that man in the Code Room is the one who's been smuggling the Russian Ice Hockey Team's game plans out of the country?" said Princess Anastasia.

"It certainly looks that way," said Fredonia. "I even saw the towels, ties, and eggs that he puts them on!"

"I'm stunned!" said Loretta.

"Ah am totally amazed," said Augusta.

"Us, too," said Carla and Marla.

"And to think that our Fredonia figured all of this out," said Miss Westminster.

Merridith started pouting.

"Hmm," said Princess Anastasia, "I wonder where my family jewels are hidden, then."

"Where's the Ukrainian egg now, Princess Anastasia?" asked Fredonia.

"It's at the hotel in a safe," said Princess Anastasia.

"Well, when we get back there, you need to take another look at it," said Fredonia. "I think we may just have this hockey game in the bag!'' She turned and walked to the door of the embassy and rang the bell.

The butler answered. ''Yes?'' he said with a sneer.

Fredonia handed him the secret file. ''Give this to the Ambassador, please,'' she said.

CHAPTER ELEVEN

And the Winner Is . . .

Long lines, twenty people deep, snaked around the Greater Moscow Fancy Ice Hockey Palace and down several blocks toward Red Square.

"Look at all those people!" said Fredonia.

"My heavens," said Miss Westminster, "there must be at least a million of them!"

"Are they all going to the ice hockey game?" asked Loretta.

"I'm sure they are," said Princess Anastasia.

"Ah've never seen so many people in all my life," said Augusta. "Not even in Atlanta!"

"I'll never be able to find my niece Olga in this crowd," said Josef, "and I was really looking forward to our reunion!"

"Hey," said Carla and Marla, "isn't that Tasha over there?"

"Where?" asked Merridith.

"That woman over there selling programs," said Carla and Marla. "That looks like Tasha!"

"It is!" said Loretta. "Hey, Tasha!" she yelled.

Tasha looked up. "Hey, girls! Vant to buy a program?"

"Sure!" said Fredonia.

Tasha rushed over with the programs. "What are you girls doing out here on the street? Aren't you supposed to be inside?"

"There's such a crowd here," said Miss Westminster, "we can't find the athletes' entrance!"

"Not to vorry," said Tasha. "Just to follow me!"

"What are you doing selling programs, Tasha?" asked Fredonia. "Why aren't you driving your taxi?"

"Are you kidding me?" said Tasha. "Everyone in Moscow is here tonight for this game. Nobody vants a taxi! I volunteered to sell programs to pick up a few rubles. Come on, I'll show you the vay to the athletes' entrance."

Tasha began walking parallel to the crowd. Everyone followed. Finally, they turned a corner, and Tasha dived into the throng of people on the sidewalk. Everyone else did the same.

"Vatch it! Vatch it!" cried the crowd. "No cuts! No cuts!"

"Is Amerikanski Ice Hockey Team!" shouted Tasha.

"Aaaaaaaaaaahhhhhhhhhhh!" sighed the crowd, then they began chanting, "You vill be smashed! You vill be smashed! You vill be smashed!"

"They wouldn't be saying that if they knew about the Ukrainian egg!" said Loretta with a smile.

"Yeah," said Fredonia.

Finally, Tasha found the athletes' entrance. She knocked three times. A door panel opened. A guard said, "You vant something?"

"Is Amerikanski Ice Hockey Team!" shouted Tasha above the chants of the crowd.

The guard opened the door and everyone rushed inside.

"Thank heavens!" said Miss Westminster. "That noise was deafening!"

"I could hardly hear myself think!" said Princess Anastasia.

"Please to take the Amerikanski Ice Hockey Team to their dressing room!" commanded Tasha.

The guard snapped to attention. "Please to follow me!" he said.

"Thanks for everything, Tasha!" shouted everyone.

"Not to mention it!" said Tasha.

"I hope you sell lots of programs," said Loretta.

"I'm doing very vell," said Tasha. "I may to give up the taxi business!"

The guard started marching down a long tunnel. Everyone waved good-bye to Tasha, then began following the guard.

When they reached the dressing room, the guard stopped, turned, then came to attention with a salute. "Please to enter!" he said.

Miss Westminster opened the door, and everyone went inside—except Josef. "Have you seen my niece, Olga?" he asked the guard.

The guard stood at ease. "You mean the Olga who used to fly but who now sells cheving gum?"

"That's the one," said Josef.

"She's sitting in the stands at this very moment," replied the guard, "Row 789, Seat AAAAAA."

Tears came to Josef's eyes. "She's my baby sister's daughter," he said, "and we're going to have a reunion. Could you please take me to her?"

"I'd to be honored!" said the guard.

The guard started marching again down the tunnel, with Josef following in step.

Miss Westminster and the girls hurriedly huddled in a circle in the dressing room. Princess Anastasia got in the middle of the circle and pulled the Ukrainian egg out of her pocket. "Okay," she said, "let's go over the Russian game plan again!"

"Pay close attention, girls!" said Miss Westminster.

"Now, after the face-off," said Princess Anastasia, "the center passes the puck to the left wing, who skates forward, then backward, then stops. He then passes the puck to the right wing, who skates laterally, then skates forward, then backward. The right wing then passes the puck back to the left wing, who does a quick wide turn, then does a quick inside turn, then passes the puck back to the right wing. The right wing does a drop pass back to the left wing, who then passes the puck back to the right wing, who then shoots. The next time the Russians get the puck, they reverse this. And that's all there is to it!''

''Have you got that, girls?'' shouted Miss Westminster.

''Yes!'' cried the girls.

''Then let's hear it!'' shouted Miss Westminster.

The girls began jumping up and down. ''We've got the egg! We've got the egg! We're going to win! We're going to win!''

Knock! Knock! Knock! Knock! Knock! Knock! Knock!

Everyone looked toward the door.

''They'll never take me alive!'' screamed Merridith.

''Please to be out on the ice rink in ten minutes!'' shouted a voice outside the door.

''Thanks,'' shouted Miss Westminster. ''We shall be!''

''You vill be smashed!'' added the voice.

''Come on, girls, let's hear it again!'' shouted Princess Anastasia.

The girls started chanting, ''We've got the egg! We've got the egg! We're going to win! We're going to win!''

''That's the spirit!'' said Miss Westminster. ''But you need to stop now and put on your uniforms and skates!''

The girls hurriedly began getting dressed.

Knock! Knock! Knock! Knock! Knock! Knock! Knock!

Merridith looked apprehensive but didn't say anything.

''Please to be out on the ice rink now!'' shouted a voice.

''We're ready!'' shouted the girls.

Miss Westminster opened the door of the dressing room. ''Come on, team!'' she cried. ''We're going to win this one for the girls of Miss Westminster's Fine School and for the fine people of Elizabeth, New Jersey!''

''Yea! Yea!'' cheered the girls.

''Oh, and one other thing,'' added Miss Westminster. She looked at Fredonia and Loretta. ''Are you two chewing gum?''

''We sure are!'' they shouted.

''Yea! Yea!'' cheered the girls again.

Everyone started walking down the tunnel toward the rink.

When they reached the ice, a deafening roar went up from the crowd.

"Good heavens!" said Miss Westminster. "Look at all those people! And there's the Ambassador holding a YOU VILL BE SMASHED pennant!"

"We'll show him!" shouted the girls.

"And look over there!" said Princess Anastasia. "It's that dear, sweet General Chekhov! He has his tanks with him!" At one end of the rink, behind the American goal, stood General Chekhov beside three Russian armored tanks. Their guns were pointed toward the center of the ice. "I think I'll go say hello," continued Princess Anastasia. "There's an important matter I've been wanting to discuss with him. Here, Miss Westminster, you hold the Ukrainian egg. I'll be right back."

Miss Westminster looked perturbed.

The referee skated over to where Miss Westminster and the girls were standing. "Places!" he shouted. "The face-off is to begin now!"

The girls skated out onto the ice and took up their positions.

Miss Westminster sat down in the team box behind the boards. A shrill whistle sounded behind her. She turned. The Minister of Sport and Mr. Malenkov were sitting together two seats up. They winked and grinned. Miss Westminster smiled weakly, then turned back toward the rink.

The game was about to begin.

Loretta stood poised in the center face-off circle opposite the seven-foot Russian center. Her eyes were on the ice.

The referee motioned to the goalies at both ends of the rink, then he dropped the puck.

Loretta controlled it.

The crowd roared, "Ooooooooooohhhhhhhhhh!" then fell silent.

Two people high up in the stands shouted, "Yea, Amerikanskis!'' It was Olga and Josef. They were sitting with their arms around each other.

But Loretta lost the puck and the crowd went wild.

The Russian center shot the puck from his defending zone through the neutral zone into the attacking zone and out of bounds.

The referee blew his whistle.

Loretta skated over to Fredonia. ''They're not doing what they're supposed to be doing,'' she said. ''They're not following the game plan on the Ukrainian egg.''

''Well, maybe they just got started off wrong,'' said Fredonia.

Loretta and the Russian center lined up for another face-off.

This time, the Russian controlled the puck.

The crowd went wild again.

The Russian center passed the puck off to the Russian left wing, who skated backward, then forward, then shot it between Fredonia's legs, scoring a goal.

''Russians one, Amerikanskis nothing!'' shouted the announcer.

The crowd stood and began stomping their feet. The building shook.

Loretta and the Russian center faced off again.

The Russian center controlled the puck.

The crowd stood again and started chanting, ''You vill be smashed! You vill be smashed! You vill be smashed!''

The buzzer sounded.

It was the end of the first period.

The crowd cheered wildly.

The girls all skated over to Miss Westminster.

''What are we going to do?'' said Fredonia frantically. ''They're not using the game plan on the Ukrainian egg!''

''I'll tell you what we're going to do,'' said Merridith, ''we're going to lose!''

89

"No, we're not!" said Miss Westminster. But she looked worried.

"Did anybody think to bring the tape of Beethoven's Concerto Number Five?" asked Augusta.

"I did," said Miss Westminster, "but I was hoping we wouldn't have to use it."

"Is it the Atlanta Symphony's version?" asked Augusta.

"No, it's the Moscow Symphony's version," said Miss Westminster.

"Well, that's it, then," said Merridith solemnly. "We've lost this game for sure!"

"Now, wait a minute, girls," said Miss Westminster. "You can't give up! We wouldn't be this far if we weren't good!"

"We're not supposed to be *this* far," said Merridith. "We're supposed to be in Buffalo!"

Miss Westminster had begun to perspire. She looked over to where Princess Anastasia was standing with General Chekhov. They were holding hands. "I wonder if Princess Anastasia would take the tape up to the sound booth for us," she said.

"We doubt it," said Carla and Marla. "We think she's gone over to the other side!"

"Never!" said Miss Westminster. "It must be part of a greater plan!"

"Well, we'd better hurry up and do something," said Loretta. "We're behind and the second period is just about to start."

Fredonia let out a shrill whistle.

Princess Anastasia looked up.

The girls motioned for her to come over.

When Princess Anastasia arrived, Miss Westminster said, "We've got a slight problem here. The Russians aren't using the game plan on the Ukrainian egg."

"Well, I wondered what was happening out there," said Princess Anastasia. She let out a big sigh. "This is really depressing. I can't believe I misread that egg again!"

90

"Well, don't worry about it," said Miss Westminster. "We've decided to use our Beethoven Concerto Number Five game plan. It has to work! But we need your help."

"You got it!" said Princess Anastasia.

Miss Westminster took the cassette tape out of her purse. "We need you to take this up to the sound booth and give it to the sound engineer," she said. "Tell him we want it for background music."

"What if he says no?" said Princess Anastasia.

"Tell him it's in the interest of international peace," said Miss Westminster.

"Then it's as good as done!" said Princess Anastasia. "I'll be right back."

They all watched as Princess Anastasia disappeared into the huge crowd, then Miss Westminster said, "We've got our work cut out for us, girls, because as soon as the Russian team hears the concerto, they'll know we've gone back to our original game plan. But remember, we're only going to try to score goals when the orchestra plays F sharp, not high C. You got that?"

"Yes!" cried the girls.

"Then let's hear it!" shouted Miss Westminster.

The girls started chanting, "We've got the tape! We've got the tape! We're going to win! We're going to win!"

"Let's start humming the concerto, girls," said Miss Westminster, "so it will be fresh in our minds when we get out onto the ice!"

All the girls began humming the concerto, except Fredonia, who had picked up the Ukrainian egg and was turning it over and over in her hands.

"Please to be on the ice immediately!" shouted the referee.

All the girls began skating out onto the ice, except Fredonia, who shouted, "I've got it! I've got it!"

"Got *what*, Fredonia?" said Miss Westminster.

"I've got the Russian game plan!" said Fredonia breathlessly. "It was on the Ukrainian egg all the time, but Princess Anastasia was holding the egg upside down, so she read the game plan backward!"

"Please to be out on the ice immediately!" screamed the referee at Fredonia.

"Time out! Time out!" shouted Miss Westminster.

"No time out! No time out!" shouted the referee.

"Oh dear, oh dear, Fredonia," said Miss Westminster, "we don't have time to learn the *real* Russian game plan. We'll just have to stick with Beethoven!"

"But . . . but . . . but . . ." Fredonia was saying as Miss Westminster pushed her out onto the ice.

"Just start humming the concerto, Fredonia," said Miss Westminster, "and everything will be all right."

Fredonia started humming. She joined the other girls, who were also humming.

"Keep humming, girls!" shouted Miss Westminster. "We've got it made!"

"Maybe not," said Princess Anastasia.

Miss Westminster turned. She was staring into a grim-faced Princess Anastasia. "What do you mean, 'maybe not'? Please don't tell me that the sound engineer refused to play the Beethoven tape!"

"Oh, he'll play it all right," said Princess Anastasia, "but at three times the normal speed."

"What?" screamed Miss Westminster. "But we didn't hum it at three times the normal speed!"

"I know," said Princess Anastasia, "but he said that was the only way he could stand to listen to Beethoven!"

"Time out! Time out!" screamed Miss Westminster at the referee.

"No time out! No time out!" screamed the referee back.

Miss Westminster looked helplessly around the Greater Moscow Fancy Ice Hocky Palace, then slowly sank down into her seat.

"Well, I think that dear, sweet General Chekhov is beginning to miss me," said Princess Anastasia. "If you'll excuse me, I'll just . . ."

"You're excused," said Miss Westminster slowly.

The referee blew his whistle.

Loretta took her place in the center face-off circle opposite the seven-foot Russian, but this time, instead of looking down at the ice, she looked him straight in the eyes and growled. The Russian was surprised—so surprised, in fact, that when the referee dropped the puck, his hockey stick missed it and Loretta took control.

Josef and Olga stood up and cheered.

The Beethoven tape began. At three times the normal speed.

Miss Westminster buried her head and began sobbing uncontrollably.

Loretta skated forward, then backward, then did a quick turn, then bumped into Augusta.

"Keep up with the music, Loretta!" shouted Augusta as she picked herself up off the ice.

"I'm trying!" Loretta shouted back.

Carla found the puck and propelled it to Augusta.

Augusta skated laterally, then forward, then backward, then ran into Merridith, who fell down in front of the Russian left wing.

Loretta picked up the puck, did a quick wide turn, then propelled it toward the Russian goal.

"That wasn't F sharp!" hissed Merridith as she got up off the ice. "You're two bars off!"

But the Russian goalie deflected the puck to the Russian left defense, who propelled it down the ice to the Russian right wing.

Carla took it away and shot it to Marla, who ran into Loretta, who fell down on the ice.

"Watch it, Loretta!" yelled Carla. "You made me miss F sharp!"

"That wasn't F sharp!" shouted Loretta as she picked herself up off the ice. "That was E flat!"

Carla whirled around, throwing up shards of ice. "Are you telling me I don't recognize an F sharp when I hear it?"

Marla whizzed by. "Quit arguing, you two. You just missed two F sharps!"

Augusta stopped the puck as it went between her legs and shot it to Merridith.

Merridith faked a pass, then shot the puck toward the Russian goal.

But the Russian left wing deflected it to the Russian right wing, who did a quick inside move, then bumped into Merridith, who bumped into Loretta, who bumped into Marla, who bumped into Augusta, who bumped into Carla, who bumped into Fredonia, who fell into the net with the puck.

"Russians two, Amerikanskis nothing!" screamed the announcer.

The buzzer sounded.

It was the end of the second period.

The crowd in the Greater Moscow Fancy Ice Hockey Palace went wild.

The girls slowly picked themselves up off the ice and skated over to where Miss Westminster was still sobbing uncontrollably.

"We're sorry, Miss Westminster," said the girls, near tears themselves.

"Ah was humming all the time Ah was out there," said Augusta, "but it didn't do any good!"

"Oh, girls, girls," sobbed Miss Westminster, "it wasn't your fault, it wasn't your fault. I just had no idea that anybody could possibly want to desecrate the music of Beethoven like that!"

The girls looked puzzled.

Miss Westminster dabbed the tears from her eyes. "Sit

down, girls," she said. "We need to talk. There's only one thing left for us to do."

"Forfeit the game?" said Loretta.

"No," said Miss Westminster calmly.

"Use the *real* Ukrainian egg game plan?" said Fredonia.

"No, not even that," said Miss Westminster.

"Well, *what*, then?" said Augusta. "Ah simply cannot stand all this suspense!"

"We are just going to go back out onto the ice and play hockey," said Miss Westminster. "That's all."

"Well, what is it you think we were doing during the first two periods?" said Merridith.

"Well, we weren't playing ice hockey, that's for sure," said Miss Westminster. "We've been trying to steal game plans and use gimmicks. We didn't get where we are now by doing that! We're a great team! We know how to play ice hockey! We're going to use our *own* game plan and go out there and win!"

The girls stood up and cheered. "We're going to win! We're going to win! We're going to win! We're going to win!"

The buzzer sounded.

"This is it, girls," said Miss Westminster. "Back out onto that ice! And Loretta and Fredonia, make sure you chew that gum harder!"

The girls skated back out onto the ice.

The puck was put into play again, but this time the Russian center controlled it. He used a backhand shot to send it to the Russian left wing, who used a forehand shot to send it to the Russian right wing. The Russian right wing used a wrist snap shot to propel the puck toward the American goal, but Fredonia knocked it away. The Russian right wing picked it up and propelled it toward the Russian left wing, but Loretta intercepted it and started moving. She skated laterally, then forward, then backward, then shot the puck to Merridith.

Merridith did some quick inside stickwork, then shot the puck to Augusta, who slap-shot it toward the Russian goal.

It went in.

"Russians two, Amerikanskis one!" gasped the announcer.

Josef and Olga stood up and cheered.

The Minister of Sport and Mr. Malenkov stopped whistling and winking.

Princess Anastasia squeezed General Chekhov's hand. He squeezed back.

Miss Westminster looked stunned.

Loretta and the Russian center returned to the center face-off.

Loretta growled again. But this time the Russian only laughed. He was still laughing when the referee dropped the puck, and Loretta controlled it again. She shot it to Augusta, who passed it to Merridith, who passed it back to Augusta. Augusta did a flip pass over the Russian left wing's stick, then shot the puck toward the Russian goal.

It went in.

"Russians two, Amerikanskis two!" cried the announcer. He was near tears.

The crowd booed angrily.

Loretta and the Russian center returned to the center face-off. The Russian's nostrils were flared. His teeth were bared. And strange sounds were coming from his throat.

The referee dropped the puck and the Russian controlled it. He shot it down the ice to the Russian left wing, who did a drop pass to the Russian right wing, who was poke-checked and lost it.

Loretta picked it up and shot it to Merridith, who shot it to Augusta, who did an inside turn, then began headmanning. Augusta shot it to Carla, who flipped it over the Russian right wing's stick to Marla, who shot it toward the Russian goal.

But the Russian goalie deflected it.

The crowd began screaming.

The Russian center picked it up and fed it to the Russian left wing, who lost it to Loretta.

The crowd booed angrily.

Loretta cut back, then broke out, then made a back diagonal pass to Marla, who fed the puck to Augusta. Augusta missed it, but Carla picked it up and passed it to Merridith.

Merridith shot it toward the Russian goal.

It went in.

"Amerikanskis three, Russians two!" sobbed the announcer uncontrollably.

The buzzer sounded.

The game was over!

There was deadly silence in the Greater Moscow Fancy Ice Hockey Palace—except for the girls, who were screaming and jumping up and down on the ice.

They finally skated over to a stunned Miss Westminster, who had now been joined by a jubilant Princess Anastasia and General Chekhov.

"Vhat a game!" cried General Chekhov.

"Thanks!" said the girls.

"Thanks!" said Miss Westminster.

"I to see that you are now coaching ice hockey instead of teaching school," said General Chekhov to Miss Westminster.

"Uh, well, uh, yes, I am!" stammered Miss Westminster.

The Ambassador rushed up. "I knew you'd win! I knew you'd win! I knew you'd win!"

But everybody ignored him, and he went away.

Over the public-address system, the funeral march had begun to play. The crowd began filing out solemnly.

"I have an announcement to make," said Princess Anastasia.

"What is it?" asked Miss Westminster.

"General Chekhov and I are planning to get married!" said Princess Anastasia.

"That's wonderful!" screamed the girls.

"Isn't this kind of sudden?" said Miss Westminster.

"It's a long story," said Princess Anastasia. "Anyway, do you remember that spot on my Ukrainian egg that I thought was a periwinkle?"

"I remember," said Fredonia. "I thought it looked like the center of an ice hockey rink."

"That's right," said Princess Anastasia, "and it turns out that you were correct! Well, I have now decided that my family jewels must be buried under the center face-off circle of this very building!"

"Really?" exclaimed everyone.

"Yes," said Princess Anastasia. She looked lovingly at General Chekhov. "And in order to recover my precious jewels, this sweetie pie here has promised that as a wedding present to me, he is going to blow up the center face-off circle with his tanks just as soon as all the people are out of the building!"

General Chekhov turned toward everyone and grinned.

CHAPTER TWELVE

The Flight Home

"It's strictly a *mariage de convenance,*" said Princess Anastasia to Miss Westminster and the girls. They were in the Pan American departure lounge at the Moscow airport, waiting for the flight to New York. "Oh, I'm sure I'll learn to love him," Princess Anastasia continued, "but right now, I just need somebody who has the means to blow up any place here in Russia where I think my jewels might be hidden. I still think there's more to that Ukrainian egg than meets the eye!"

"I'm sorry you didn't find your jewels under the center face-off circle at the Greater Moscow Fancy Ice Hockey Palace," said Fredonia.

"So am I," said Princess Anastasia.

"Boy, that place sure was a mess after General Chekhov's tanks got through with it, wasn't it?" said Loretta.

"Yes, it was," said Princess Anastasia. There was a gleam in her eye.

"Special Pan American charter flight for New York is now ready for departure. Please to come aboard!"

"That voice sounds familiar," said Augusta.

Everyone hugged and kissed Princess Anastasia, then hurried down the tunnel to the airplane.

Olga and Josef were standing at the door. They were dressed in Pan American flight attendant uniforms.

"Velcome aboard!" shouted Olga. Josef fell to his knees.

"Ah thought Ah recognized that voice," said Augusta.

"What are you two doing here?" asked Merridith.

"Vell, Pan American vas looking for an experienced flight attendant, so I applied for the job," said Olga. "Naturally they vanted to hire me. But I told them I vouldn't to take the job unless they offered Uncle Josef one, too!"

Josef stood up. "My job is to pretend to fix the toilets," he said. "I'm glad that I'll be able to use my training."

"Well, congratulations!" said Miss Westminster.

"Yeah, congratulations!" echoed the girls.

Olga showed them all to their seats and gave them pillows and blankets.

"I am at peace with myself," said Fredonia as she curled up into her seat. "I have accepted the fact that I am one of the greatest hockey players in the history of the game!"

"It really is hard to be humble when you're world champions, isn't it?" said Merridith.

"Ah don't want to see another hockey puck as long as Ah live," said Augusta.

"Us, either," said Carla and Marla.

"I doubt if you will have to, girls," said Miss Westminster. "After all, who else is there in the world left to play?"

"When you're the best, you're the best," said Loretta. "That's all there is to it."

"Miss Vestminster, vould you like to read *The New York Times?*" said Olga. "Is only two days old!"

"Thanks," said Miss Westminster as Olga handed her the newspaper. *"Aaaaaiiiiieeeee!"*

The girls threw off their blankets and rushed to Miss Westminster's side.

"What's the matter?" asked Fredonia.

"Look at the headlines!" gasped Miss Westminster.

Everyone looked: "Miss Choate's Fine School for Girls of Buffalo Scores Upset Victory Over American Men's Ice Hockey Team, Claims World Championship!"

"What are we going to do?" sobbed Loretta.

"We're going to settle this once and for all," said Miss Westminster. She stood up. "Olga!" she shouted. "Tell the pilot to take this plane to Buffalo!"

Olga saluted, then did a Cossack dance toward the cockpit.

"Josef!" shouted Miss Westminster.

Josef came running down the aisle. "Yes, Miss Westminster?"

"Have the copilot radio a message to Miss Choate at Miss Choate's Fine School for Girls of Buffalo, New York!" shouted Miss Westminster.

Josef saluted, took out a pad and pen, then fell to his knees. "What's the message?" he asked.

Miss Westminster set her jaw and took a deep breath. *"You vill be smashed!"* she roared.

A CAST OF CHARACTERS TO DELIGHT THE HEARTS OF READERS!

BUNNICULA   51094-4/$2.50
James and Deborah Howe, illustrated by Alan Daniel
The now-famous story of the vampire bunny, this ALA Notable Book begins the light-hearted story of the small rabbit the Monroe family find in a shoebox at a Dracula film. He looks like any ordinary bunny to Harold the dog. But Chester, a well-read and observant cat, is suspicious of the newcomer, whose teeth strangely resemble fangs…

HOWLIDAY INN   69294-5/$2.50
James Howe, illustrated by Lynn Munsinger
"Another hit for the author of BUNNICULA!"
                                            School Library Journal
The continued "tail" of Chester the cat and Harold the dog as they spend their summer vacation at the foreboding Chateau Bow-Wow, a kennel run by a mad scientist!

THE CELERY STALKS AT MIDNIGHT   69054-3/$2.50
James Howe, illustrated by Leslie Morrill
Bunnicula is back and on the loose in this third hilarious novel featuring Chester the cat, Harold the dog, and the famous vampire bunny. This time Bunnicula is missing from his cage, and Chester and Harold turn sleuth to find him, and save the town from a stalk of bloodless celery! "Expect surprises. Plenty of amusing things happen."
                                      The New York Times Book Review

AVON Camelot Paperbacks

Avon Camelot Books are available at your bookstore. Or, you may use Avon's special mail order service. Please state the title and code number and send with your check or money order for the full price, plus $1.00 per copy to cover postage and handling, to: AVON BOOK MAILING SERVICE, P.O. Box 690, Rockville Centre, NY 11571

Please allow 6-8 weeks for delivery.